TWO HURTLED GLOVES

Two Hurtled Gloves

Byron James-Adams

Two Hurtled Gloves
Copyright @ 2024 by James Byron Books

www.jamesbyronbooks.com
ISBN
978-0-9756684-0-5 (Paperback)
978-0-9756684-1-2 (eBook)

This story is fictitious.
Some long-standing institutions, agencies, and public offices do exist.
The characters and situations involved are wholly imaginary, and resemblance to natural persons, living or dead, or actual events is purely coincidental.

Again a big thanks to my beta readers. You know who you are...

Cover Art: Canva by author.
Internal Book Design: Ingram Sparks.

Welcome back to Nic Thorn & Associates' world of diversions and distractions which begins on a golden beach in Port Douglas, tracks down to Tasmania, and up to the banks of Brisbane. The Team has to investigate a wedded miss, the misguided pretence of Tiger tracking, and banking blasphemy.

Site Locations:

1. Brisbane (Book 1) - One Tricked Phoney
2. Adelaide (Book 1) - One Tricked Phoney
3. Pinnaroo (Book 1) - One Tricked Phoney
4. Port Douglas (Book 2) - Two Hurtled Gloves
5. Corrina (Book 2) - Two Hurtled Gloves
6. Brisbane (Book 2) - Two Hurtled Gloves

CHAPTER 1

Rosemary Palmer was standing on a large wrap-around balcony of a holiday apartment at the Sea Temple Resort, Port Douglas, Far North Queensland. The beautiful Four Mile Beach stretched out below her, and yachts with full billowed sails were plying the crystal blue water of the bay, but she was not interested in any of it as she was here to get married. Again.

The last time she stood at the altar, she was to marry a short, fat, and shallow man named Michael because her father needed to secure one of his business deals, and as a nineteen-year-old, she was the sacrificial lamb. The deal fell over in a week, and the marriage lasted less than that. Rose still remembers the endless arguments with her father: 'I'm still so young, and at uni, Father for God's sake. I can't love him. I don't even like him. Can't you offer up a couple of your luxury cars instead? Please.'

Her parents put it down to pre-wedding jitters, but Rose wanted to put herself down with a handful of sleeping tablets and a large glug of Glen Fiddich. The marriage ceremony went through, and she had still not forgiven them some ten years later. Rose took a deep breath, considered that she had no choice but to go through with it, and called out to Sandy, her BFF, and bridesmaid: 'Sandy, can we go for a walk, please? There is still a while before I need to prepare for this thing. Can I at least enjoy my last few moments of singledom looking at something beautiful?'

They went down to the beach and were amused by all the warning signs: 'Caution – Danger – Stingers, Sharks & Crocodiles are in the water.' Rose looked at Sandy. 'So maybe today isn't the day I go for a swim.'

A while later, they returned to the apartment and Rose was finally ready; 'I'm dressed as a lemon meringue pie. I can't wear this. Who chose it anyway?'

Sandy responded quickly: 'Nic Thorn.'

'Damn you, Nic. I have already given up so much for him. I got soggy and gawked at by a posse of schoolboys after pirouetting through a waterfall in Brisbane. I was held up at broom point during a robbery in outback Pinnaroo in South Australia, but no, now he wants me to get married dressed as a fluffy yellow and white tart.'

Sandy rolled her blonde hair into a bouffant and secured it with pearl inlaid clips, then helped Rose with the veil. 'You know, I would have been his bride if he asked me, but I'm a blonde and can't wear yellow.' Rose was finally convinced to overcome her reluctance, and they headed toward the ceremony. Apart from the wedding party, it helped that no one else in Port Douglas knew them.

Sandy nodded toward the assembled group. 'Oh, by the way, your brother won't be able to make it up from Hobart as it is fogged in, but he took great delight in telling me that your parents couldn't manage to get a flight up from Brisbane, either. They are furious that you didn't invite them to their only daughter's latest wedding.' Rose pushed a recalcitrant lock of her brunette hair back under the veil, held her head a little higher and continued.

As the duo stepped into the beautiful sunshine, it was another perfect day in Far North Queensland. Birds were chirping, leaf blowers bellowing, and the errant dog was barking at no one in particular. Rose took a deep breath and trudged her way over the lush green grass to the wedding gazebo set up for them in the Sea Temple's gardens.

'Please don't trudge, Rose. A bride should be elegant, sunny, and beautiful. It is her day of all days.'

'I can't help it, Sandy. It's stinking hot, and the air is so humid you could slice it. Besides, this damn buffalo grass is so lush; you *could* lose a buffalo in it.'

Rose suddenly stopped as she looked at the wedding party waiting for her at the makeshift altar, causing Sandy to almost run into her. The small crowd was eager for the ceremony to begin, so the Celebrant smiled at Rose and gave her a nod, which was enough for Rose to start to turn around.

Sandy saw Rose's look of panic and prevented her from escaping. 'C'mon, it's not like you haven't done it before. Oops, sorry, that wasn't nice. Let's say the first one was the rehearsal, and this *is* the real thing this time.'

Rose muttered: 'I can do this, I can do this, but it's not like baking a cake. I'm dressed as a big fluffy lemon meringue pie. Here comes the bride, all fat and wide.' Sandy nodded to the Celebrant; 'Sshh. You're keeping Nic waiting.'

Just then Billy Idol's song 'Nice Day for White Wedding' started blaring from the audio speakers. Rose looked at Sandy, then to Nic waiting at the altar, and whispered; 'Damn you again, Nic.'

The music was altered, and Mendelsohn's traditional bridal march was played, much to Rose's preference, so she gathered her courage, stepped back in sync with the music, and they stopped in front of the Celebrant. Rose took hold of the groom's hand and looked over to Nic.

The waiting crowd stood up to welcome the bride and her maid of honour, however, there was a slight delay as the group had to wait for the gardener to turn off his lawnmower. He made his way to an empty chair, removed his hat and gloves, and bowed an apology to the wedding party. Those in attendance sat down, and the ceremony began. Nic gave Rose a subtle smile.

The Celebrant stood at the lectern and began:

'Dearly beloved, we are gathered here today in the presence of friends and family to witness the joining of this bride and groom in holy matrimony... if there is anyone here today that objects to the bringing together of this couple, please speak now or forever after hold your peace...'

Rose took a breath and looked at Nic, and then a cry came from the crowd. It was a woman's voice. She was standing in the aisle and waving her hand. 'Excuse me, excuse me, but I do have an objection to these proceedings...'

Nic, Rose, Sandy, and the groom turned towards the woman, and the Celebrant glared in the direction of the interruption. 'I am sorry, madam, why shouldn't this wedding proceed? Please state your name and the basis of the delay.'

'Certainly, my name is Detective Kate Jenkins. On behalf of the South Australian Police and in conjunction with the Queensland Police, I hereby charge you with one count of Social Security Fraud and another of breaching the Marriage Act. These indictments are sufficient to hold you pending further investigations.'

Suddenly, a large yellow leathered gardening glove was thrown from the crowd, which landed with a plop in front of the wedding party. Meantime, another woman had stood up.

'You toad, you're not even a registered Celebrant. Nate and I spent the last six months thinking we'd been married, all for nothing. We had to go through it all over again, and I wasn't....we weren't supposed to be together before marriage.'

A third woman stood up and threw the second gardening glove, and her attempt was more successful as it smacked the Celebrant directly in the face.

'You are a mongrel. We're even taking marriage counselling to try and come to terms with all this, too.'

The Celebrant looked at the Detective, then at Nic, turned and bolted. The sound technician decided to follow the lead of the decamped celebrant, and the groom watched as the two people ran away, and then looked toward the Detective.

'And I guess I'm in trouble too, Detective Jenkins?'

'Yes, Dr Garden, please stay here. We'll be taking you in for questioning, too,' then looked over to Nic. 'We'd better go after them. They're heading to the beach. Do you know if they have a boat? Are they that organised?'

Nic shrugged his shoulders. 'Maybe.'

Meantime, Rose and Sandy were taking a seat on the gazebo steps as the groom loosened his tie and walked up to them. 'When did you know it was a scam, ladies? I mean, look at me and look at you. You both look like you've fallen out of the latest Wedding magazine. I thought this was all happening too quickly, but the Celebrant assured me it was all legitimate. I had even paid him the two thousand with another thousand due in a week. I still haven't got my Australian Citizenship yet either.'

Rose nodded. 'Yes, it is a wedding scam, Graham. We have been following them for about six months.'

The groom sighed and sat down. 'Do you mind if I take off my suit jacket now?' Rose nodded again. 'Sure, it is a bit warm.'

The groom removed his coat, top hat and gloves, then he removed a toupee and put it all beside him. They were sitting silently when Rose noticed movement behind her: 'I think your hat is moving, Graham.'

Graham looked behind him as a white Ibis had taken the toupee in its beak and tried to pull it away from under the top hat. He growled at it to let go, then grabbed at the wig. It was now a tug-of-war between the bird and the older man. The bird was winning and Sandy stifled a laugh at the commotion. 'Looks like your tug-of-war buddy has reinforcements coming in.' A couple of white Ibis had joined in with the fracas, and even two crows had flown down to await their turn for the supposed tasty morsel. There were now three Ibis tugging against him. Graham stood up. 'Come on, ladies. I'm too old for this. Please help me.'

They looked at him, stood up, and started to flap their arms. It was now three against three, but suddenly, the wig tore in half, and Graham was thrown backward. Rose managed to keep him from falling back off the stage. They watched the determined Ibis take flight with its supposed morsel. Graham shrugged his shoulders and placed his torn half into his pocket. 'That was my favourite one too.' They all sat back down on the steps, exhausted from the battle of the lost toupee. Half of it, anyway.

In the meantime, down at the beach, Nic and Detective Jenkins had arrived and watched as the two escaping men leapt into a waiting boat. It quickly motored away, and the Detective stopped running. 'I think we just missed them, Nic.'

'Not exactly, Kate.'

The boat suddenly did a 180-degree turn, grounded itself high upon the shore, and the driver jumped out. 'Two hundred cash, you said. I waited for ten minutes. A good day's pay just for that.'

Kate and Nic waited whilst the boat driver jogged away. 'How did you know? How did you know they wouldn't simply keep going?'

'He was one of my guys. I mean, they would've checked the boat, but you'd think they would've checked that it was their driver?' Kate went up the boat and looked at the two escapees. 'Give it up, guys.' Nic walked over to a 'Caution – Danger in the water' sign, pulled it out of the ground, and held it towards the two men: 'Your choice, guys. Either come with us or take your chances in the water.'

The men looked at each other, climbed out of the boat, and were led back along the path to the grounds of the Sea Temple to be helped into the waiting Police wagon. Kate and the Sergeant climbed into the front, and they drove off.

Nic then went over to Sandy and Rose, giving them both a hand to rise, but suddenly jumped in shock as a woolly brown lump of discarded fluff landed on his shoulder. 'Cripes, I'm hit. I'm hit.' Nic stopped mid-dance, removed it, and handed it back to Graham. 'Sorry, mate. I didn't realise these things can attack you too.'

Graham nodded, pulled the half from his pocket, put both halves of the toupee together on his head, and firmly plopped the top hat back on. Sandy looked at Nic as they watched him walk away. 'So Nic, always a bridesmaid, never a bride?'

'Not really, it's your turn next. Anyway, it's pretty humid out here, and Rose, thanks for being my bride, seeing it was such short notice.'

Nic then stepped back onto the steps to address the crowd: 'The show is over, and thanks for coming. Can I suggest you go to the bar? Drinks are on me.'

One of the ladies from the crowd came up. 'See you in about an hour at the next one.' The small group disbanded and chairs were collected.

Rose and Sandy gathered their belongings and went to the kerb where a dark limousine awaited. They stepped inside and each took a bottle of water from the bar. Rose nodded to the driver. 'Thanks for waiting, Elle. How long is the drive to Cairns?'

The driver pushed the button to lower the partition

screen. 'Only about half an hour, but you have about ten minutes to change. Nic says we must be there on time to meet the next groom and ensure you read the background file brief. It's on the seat and has the names of the people at the wedding party.'

Sandy and Rose quickly changed into their new outfits, and just as they finished, Nic opened the door. 'Let's go, Elle.' The driver moved into the traffic, and their group headed off.

They were about ten minutes into the ride when Sandy pushed the button for the driver's intercom. 'Elle, can you please turn up the air-conditioning? It's pretty warm dressed in this pretty...um...It's not pretty at all. What exactly am I dressed in, Nic?'

Rose was helping Sandy don a sizeable red wig. 'I think the outfit is from an early 'Bride of Franken-stein' movie. The brief says the groom, apart from having the first name of Frank, has a surname of Stein. I assume his middle initial is an 'N.'

Nic nodded in confirmation whilst Sandy wobbled her head to settle into the new hairdo, and she con-tinued. 'So Nic, is my middle initial 'N' for Nannette or Nancy? Can I guess? Nincompoop? For allowing you to get us involved in this scam?'

Nic looked at her. 'You know I didn't have time to settle on your names for this one. Let's call you Nellie and Rose; you be Ellie.'

Rose shook her head. 'Surely you put someone's name on the driver's marriage application form?'

Nic shook his head. 'Actually, no...that's all part of the scam that these guys are running. They complete the marriage registration after the event.'

Sandy nodded toward the driver. 'You can't use Ellie...it's our driver's name, which might confuse the groom.'

The driver responded. 'It's OK, Sandy. The 'Elle' is for the letter 'L' as in Limousine driver. Oh, and it looks like we're here.' DriverL pulled the car to a stop outside the new Cairns Aquarium as a space had been allocated for them with duly decorated witches' hats, and the gathered crowd clapped the group. They went inside towards the 400,000-litre fish tank where the wedding party awaited. The groom was dressed as a Frankenstein, including a cardboard boxed head from which black hair dye was dripping.

Rose looked at him and whispered to Sandy: 'I think he's melting.'

Nic moved forward to address the small crowd. 'Sorry, we're late. The bride had to stop for a quick bite. The child is recovering well, though.'

The crowd chortled at his comment.

Nic then nodded to the Celebrant, and the music started. It was the theme from the movie 'Jaws.' Sandy stepped into time with the music, and the process began, but this time, when it got to the part about *'Does anyone here object to this couple joining in holy matrimony?...'* Rose put her hand up and the Celebrant looked at her. 'Yes, I'm sorry this marriage can't proceed. You love someone else, don't you, Ellie?' Sandy realised she'd forgotten to read the brief thoroughly. 'Um...yes I do...oops...that's not the right thing to say, is it?'

The Celebrant looked at Sandy. 'Well, do you love someone else, Ellie? Do you, Ellie?'

The crowd leaned forward, listening eagerly for her reply.

'Yes, I'm .....' Sandy was trying to think of a response when Detective Kate finally arrived: 'Stop this. It is a wedding scam. Everyone stay where you are.'

Sandy whispered to Rose, then nodded to the Hammerhead shark circling slowly within the tank. 'That was lucky. The only name I came up with was Feargal Sharkey.'

The Celebrant looked at Nic, then towards the groom. 'Sorry everybody, I need to be somewhere else.' He gathered his papers, quickly ascended the stairs, and headed for the nearest exit.

Nic looked over to Kate. 'Not again....'

CHAPTER 2

Kate and Nic gave chase, and the rest of the Rent-A-Crowd joined this time whilst Frank Stein, Sandy, and Rose remained where they were to watch the calamity unfold. Frank finally spoke: 'I thought it was a scam. I mean, how often do they have weddings in here anyway?'

Rose looked at him. 'Is that the only thing that led you to this conclusion? What about the fact that you don't even know the name of the woman you are supposed to marry.'

'Well, there is that too.'

They continued to watch the Celebrant try to evade the melee. He'd finally given up running in circles and dove into the open top of the large fish tank.

Rose smiled as they watched the man floundering in the water, then she picked up a piece of paper, wrote something on it in lipstick, and held it up against the glass for him to read: 'Watch out for the Piranhas.'

Nic and Kate recovered the soggy escapee from the aquarium and led him outside to the waiting Police Van.

Meanwhile, Rose and Sandy returned to their car, and were getting changed when the door opened, and Nic stepped in. 'Two down, two to go.' DriverL checked that everyone was buckled in and headed toward Mackay, about an eight-hour drive.

Around four hours later, they decided to have a stopover in the town of Ayr, and Rose seemed to be taking a long time to return from collecting the supplies. Nic checked his watch. 'If Rose doesn't come out in the next couple of minutes, I think we'll give the next one a miss.'

Sandy turned to face him. 'Really? I'm already over this wedding thing.'

'Not likely. We're in the middle of the 'Wacky Whitsunday Wedding' season, so it's open slather up here. We've got two to go, but the next one is big.'

'How big?'

'It's all three of us getting married this time. It's one of those weddings where multiple couples are getting hitched, and at last count, it was at least seven couples, three dogs, a cat, a goldfish, and a little pink pony.'

Sandy shook her head. 'How's that going to work? Are you marrying both of us?'

Nic grinned. 'Yep, I've been studying to become a polygamist. I believe it's legal in some parts of America. I'll have to change my religion.'

Sandy looked at him. 'Are you a Catholic, Uniting, or Baptist?'

'Wheelbarrow.'

'What's that? I've never heard of it.'

'It means I only go to church when I'm pushed.'

Sandy punched him softly in the arm. 'Mind you, I'm a great fan of the Aussie band, The Church. I was in my early twenties when we saw them play at the Sydney Opera House in April 2011.'

Nic nodded in confirmation. 'Their best song was found 'Under the Milky Way' and I must play that one next time I get a chance. It's another great song based on four chords. I should be able to remember that even though I'm getting old.'

Rose finally emerged from the restaurant. 'Kate has just filled me in on these marriage scams. Some of the scammers are using them as their full-time employ-ment. It's a national network of unwelcome wedding wizardry.'

Nic smiled. 'I know, and we're only looking at the tip of the iceberg, or the cake's topping as the case may be, but we've got to get down to the town of Mackay for the next one. It starts at midnight tonight.'

They returned to the car and headed toward Mackay.

It was close to midnight when they finally arrived and had managed to catch up on some sleep during the drive. Nic was in the process of changing his shirt but was taking a long time to put a fresh one on. He decided to sit there shirtless whilst he struggled to remove the pins and papers from the shirt packet.

DriverL called out. 'Please put your shirt back on, Nic. It's causing a glare in my rear-view mirror.'

Nic bowed as best he could and put his shirt on. 'Fair enough, but I am almost a married man, so I shouldn't be in the back of a limousine with two single ladies. Besides that, how did I miss my Buck's Night?'

Sandy grinned. 'You slept through it. You're nearly forty, you know.'

'Thanks for the reminder. I might sit here, close my eyes, and think about what I'll miss out on now that I've given up my singledom.' Nic shut his eyes momentarily. 'Wow, I didn't miss much.'

The group finally arrived at the foreshore, and DriverL drove onto the beach. 'It's OK guys, I've got permission,' then headed for the site where a well-lit stage was set up along with a group of similarly dressed Celebrants waiting under flower-filled arches.

In front of the stage, each couple and their animals had been allocated a small, penned area of framing provided by a local farmer. The trio alighted from the vehicle, all dressed in white suits this time, and duly approached their appointed registrar.

Nic took the lead. 'Hi, I'm Jordy, and these two are my brides, Herdie and Gerdie.' The registrar reviewed his paperwork, completed the names, and then had Nic, Rose, and Sandy sign the wedding agreement. They had to acknowledge that the wedding was not being made under duress and was of sound mind. Nic noticed Rose hesitated when she was about to execute the document.

Everyone had taken their allocated pens and were waiting for the process to commence when suddenly one of the couples started arguing, and then the groom began bleating like a lost lamb. His bride glared at him. 'Stop that, Larry. This is serious as we're about to get married. I'm not going to marry you if you're going to behave like an...an old goat.'

The man yelled back at his partner. 'I was practising sounding like your mother. I told you I didn't want to do this. It's too soon.'

The woman looked at him with her mouth agape. 'Oh, no...you're not serious?'

The man continued to bait her; 'Baa, baa,' then he changed it to 'Bye, Bye', stepped out, and bowed to the others. 'Best of luck to all of you, and by the way, being a G.O.A.T doesn't always mean Greatest Of All Time.'

Meantime, Nic wasn't watching the drama unfolding as he had his own issue to contend with as Kate had not yet arrived. 'Hey guys, Kate is not here yet, so we might have to stall things a little. Is anyone up for a diversion?'

Rose looked at him. 'I won't bleat like a sheep or moo like a cow. What do you want us to do then?'

'How about one of you faints, or better yet, both of you faint....'

Sandy looked at him. 'Why don't you just ask our Celebrant to wait as we all have second thoughts?'

'That might work too.'

Nic was about to call him over when DriverL ran up, so he stepped out of the pen to talk to her. 'Kate just rang. There's a major car accident on the Bruce Highway, and she's stuck in traffic.'

'OK, thanks. Do you have any ideas how to stall all this then?'

DriverL smiled. 'I've got one. You might hear something very loud and be ready with your best-panicked face look whilst I'm setting it up.'

Nic nodded and stepped back into the pen. 'Guys, I think something big is about to happen, so be prepared....'

The marriage ceremonies were about to commence when the sound of a cyclone warning siren blared from the on-beach speakers. Then a safety narration began: *Warning, warning. This is not a drill. Warning. A Cyclone has been forecasted in this immediate vicinity. Please evacuate. Evacuate now.'*

Nic smiled, then whispered, 'Yep, that will work. Good job, DriverL.'

Rose and Sandy moved over to him. 'Is this for real?'

Nic looked at them. 'It's as real as it can be at such short notice.'

The crowd started moving out of their pens, and the Celebrants quickly closed off the area to move away from the beach, but no one happened to notice the wind had not picked up, nor were there clouds in the dark midnight sky.

Some of the Celebrants had returned to their vehicles and started driving to the beach access exit area, where the local Police were happy to hold them pending the arrival of Kate and her crew. A few of them tried to escape into the water, but everyone knew it was 'stinger' season, so they quickly gave up. Kate finally arrived at two-thirty in the morning and gave the Celebrants a late and great reception.

As the group was staying overnight in Mackay, Rose, Sandy, and DriverL were sound asleep when the Detective finished the paperwork at the beach, and it was well after four a.m. when she finally arrived at the hotel. Nic was still down at the front bar waiting for her. 'You took your time.'

'I know the life of a real crime fighter never rests. At least you can remove your mask and hide in plain sight; we must carry our badges in full view of the public.'

'You could come and work for me, you know.'

'How would that work? I couldn't make an arrest and I don't think calling out 'Stop, or I'll make a citizen's arrest' quite cuts it in the real world.'

Good point. We've got the last one to go, so it's back to Brisbane for us. Are you going to meet us down there?'

'Nope, you're on your own for that one. Let me know if you need help. I'm off to the airport and flying home to Adelaide. It was a good marriage whilst it lasted, but I don't think I'll tell my husband about it.'

Kate mock saluted, and Nic watched her leave, then called out: 'Until next time...when I need a bride or two or three.'

CHAPTER 3

Sandy, Rose, Nic, and DriverL were enjoying breakfast when Nic's phone rang. He stood up and walked away to take the call. DriverL watched him move out of range. 'I hate it when he does that.'

Sandy took a bite of her toast. 'How long have you worked with Nic?'

'A couple of times, but he doesn't head up this way very much anymore. He's too busy chasing down the real work. The big city stuff that pays more.'

'Like what?'

DriverL shook her head. 'Like, I don't know. I never hear what he does or where he goes. How long have you been working for him.'

Rose responded. 'We don't work for him. We follow him around like we're on an extended holiday.'

Nic returned to the table. 'OK, the next one we're going to is on one of the islands off the coast of Brisbane. Guess which one, and I'll shout the winner breakfast.'

Sandy looked at him. 'It's likely to be included in the room's tariff.'

'Oh well, at least I offered. Anyway, take a guess.'

Rose responded. 'It's on Moreton Island. There's a dog wedding ceremony thing all this weekend.' Nic nodded. 'Spoilsport.' Rose continued. 'I tried to enrol Dog, and they were excited about me coming over until I told them my dog breed was a Maine Coon cat. It was such a good deal. Three nights, breakfast included, and a sunset sailboat ride. Of course, any dogs were free of charge.'

The group left the Hotel and headed to the airport for the short flight back to Brisbane. Rose noticed the Detective had not joined up with them. 'What happened to Kate? Isn't she joining us?'

'Actually, Kate left on an earlier flight back to Adelaide. She thoroughly enjoyed her little holiday with us, too.' Rose looked at him. 'Working holiday?'

'Oh no, she was definitely on leave.'

'But she made all those arrests....'

'She did, and it's amazing how compliant people are when a real Police Badge is presented to them.' Sandy laughed. 'So, you scammed them, and they got locked up anyway?'

Nic smiled. 'Yep, they all went to the Police Station of their own accord and then were arrested.'

They drove to the airport where DriverL assisted them with the luggage to the booking area, then tapped at the brim of her chauffeur cap. 'Until next time you get up this way. It's been my pleasure driving you.'

The flight landed in Brisbane, and they returned to their homes to pack for the next wedding. As the resort reservation had been made a few weeks ago, Nic, Sandy, and Rose were ready to join the celebrations on the island but had trouble finding a suitable dog at such short notice. They tried the local pounds and rescue centres but were told there's no such thing as 'borrowing a dog for a wedding.'

They eventually rented a pair of miniature schnauzers, and Nic had to convince himself about the cost. 'I know five hundred dollars is a high price for dog sitting, after all, they are pedigrees, but I'm not quite sure what breed.'

Nic collected the dogs from the owner a few days later and headed to West End to collect Rose and Sandy. He was driving his black 300C Chrysler when he pulled into their driveway. 'The boys are in the back seat, so someone will have to sit up front with me. Come and meet 'Budd and Yzah.'' Nic opened the rear door; both dogs looked at Rose and snarled, so she stepped back. 'Do they do that a lot?'

Nic shook his head. 'Nope, only when they smell a cat, a rat, or a Matt.'

The two dogs suddenly went quiet as Dog approached to see who the visitors were. The eight-kilogram Maine Coon cat peered inside the car, gave a little 'prupp' then waddled off. Rose ignored Dog and continued to watch the two dogs as they were now cowering in the back seat. 'Can I assume they've never seen such a large cat before?'

Nic nodded again. 'I hadn't either until I met yours.'

They climbed into the car, headed off, and arrived at the Redcliffe Ferry terminal about an hour later. Nic parked in secured parking, but there was pandemonium on the other side of the fence. There were about fifteen dogs unleashed and another twenty getting tangled up on their leashes. Sandy helped wrangle some of the recalcitrant dogs whilst Rose and Nic stood back and watched.

A trio of dachshunds ran up to them, and they waited as Rose patted each one. 'So, remind me what's the scam here?' Nic nodded. 'It's about people paying to marry their dogs and how much they're paying for the service. None of it is legal, though.'

Rose nodded. 'So again, what's the scam?'

'One of the 'celebrants' claims they have the binding legal right to undertake the ceremony. They are charging up to a thousand dollars to ratify it under some foreign rule in some foreign countries, then they convince the owners to claim the animals as their spouses and gain access to additional pensions.'

Rose again nodded. 'Why don't they just stop it?'

'Who are they? We're part of the 'they'. If a government entity like Centrelink or Medicare is presented with an original marriage certificate showing a person's name, it just might get past the authorities. We'll be looking for cases like that.'

The ferry ride lasted just over half an hour, and it was mayhem again on the island.

Dogs were off their leashes, and owners ran around trying to gain control. One poor soul had volunteered to collect the doggy deposits, and everything was getting messy. Nic and Rose carried their dogs to the reception area and finalised the bookings, which included the additional fees for doggy lodgings', although some of the other dog owners frowned on their decision. Nic laughed about it afterwards. 'Hey, if you lie with dogs, you get fleas. I read that on the back of a door once, although it might've been 'if you flee with dogs, you might get lies'. Rose was subconsciously scratching her scalp, then stopped. 'So, whom do we have to find, and what should we look for?'

Nic smiled. 'Someone that believes in their importance and is as smug as a pug in a rug. There's no such thing as a legal name when naming a dog. It's just the name of the dog.'

Sandy finally caught up with them about half an hour later. 'Well, that was interesting. I've been told a couple is setting up a tent further down the beach offering a binding marriage.'

'Between dogs or between people?'

'Between a dog and a human, although the person can't be an Australian citizen, which makes sense I suppose as you still can get a foreign pension whilst you live here.'

Rose responded. 'But if you get a pension from

another country, how will they check that you haven't legitimately married in Australia? It's all rather confusing, but I'm not an expert on this marriage stuff.'

Nic nodded. 'OK, so let's leave it for a few hours and wander down there with our two dogs.'

Rose looked at him. 'Who is going to play the naïve pensioner then?'

'Well, I can use a toffy English accent if needed.' Nic attempted a Cary Grant impersonation. 'Judy, Judy, Judy. I've just lost my favourite slippers in the river.' They both looked at him, but Rose spoke first. 'I don't think that will work, but it was a good Michael Caine accent. Why don't we use the direct method?'

Nic responded again: 'R, that's what I was thinking too, me wee lassie. Make mine shaken, not stirred.'

'Was that supposed to be Sean Connery? It sounded more like Roger Moore?'

'Yep. Pretty good, hey?'

This time, Sandy shook her head. 'I think we'll be asking the questions.'

Their group headed to the lunch buffet and were watching the unfolding circus when an elderly couple came up to them, being dragged along by a pair of Great Danes. They looked at Rose. 'Where's your pooch?'

Rose quickly responded. 'We brought along a dog walker for them so we could enjoy our holiday on this beautiful island without any distractions. I don't actually like dogs.'

They looked at her. 'Really?'

Nic took over the conversation. 'No, the truth is my friend here is a Dog Catcher on holiday from Melbourne. Please don't tell anyone, especially the dogs.'

The couple then took off quickly, being led by their dogs, not because they wanted to, but because the Danes wanted to chase a seagull. Nic watched them being dragged away. 'You'd think they would get ones they can handle, not just because they like to be in charge.'

Sandy looked at him. 'I assume you're talking about the dogs?'

About an hour later, they had collected Budd and Yzah from the kennel and made their way to the tent, deciding that Nic would not ask any questions. Two other couples were reading the brochures, and a man was holding a Chow puppy. He was asking some of the questions, so Nic's group moved closer: 'So, are you saying if I change my dog's name to Julie Green and make up a date of birth, you will issue a marriage certificate, and I can legally claim her as a dependant?'

The spruiker nodded. 'When was the last time the Tax Office checked your children were no longer living from home? When my kids moved out to live with my ex, they kept claiming full dependency. I never changed her age on my tax return. She's been fifteen for three years.'

Mr Chow-man nodded. 'But that's tax fraud. Surely

it will create an anomaly when your daughter gets a Tax File Number?'

The attendant smiled smugly as he was already waiting for the response. 'Not if she gets one under a different name. She's getting married next month. So, would you like to get married to your Chow? It only costs two thousand dollars, and you can pay in four instalments, or if you pay a hundred percent, now I'll give you a twenty percent discount.'

Rose leaned in, took a brochure, and muttered under her breath but loud enough for Mr Chow-man to overhear. 'It is still fraud.'

Mr Chow-man stepped back. 'I'll think about it. Let me talk to my wife first. She makes all the decisions, including buying this dog. I'm a cat person.'

Nic then moved in. 'I'm interested. Tell me, do you also do a full wedding ceremony?' The attendant stood up quickly. 'Certainly, I can arrange that. We have three different types of ceremonies. It depends on how quickly you want it done, how quickly we can organise it, and ...How much you want to spend?'

Nic handed over a silver Credit Card. 'I think my Quantum Palladium Card will cover the expense. Let's go the whole hog.... Sorry, I meant dog.'

Rose leaned in to check out the Credit card, having never seen the brand, and muttered: 'Shiny.'

The man took a few notes, then introduced his business associate to complete the formalities: 'I'm Meg Fountaine. Thank you for choosing the services of 'Evvisa gli sposi'- Long Live the Bride and Groom.' The young woman smiled and led Nic's group to another tent behind them.

'So, can you please confirm your name and address? Are you an Australian citizen, and what is the name of the prospective spouse? Oh, and when and where would you like to be married?'

Nic nodded. 'My name is Nicllaus Szertkovic. I was born in Lovinkia and currently live there. It is one of the new Balkan States. We're on holiday.'

The assistant opened a laptop and began entering the data. 'Do you have a residential address in Lovinkia?'

Rose nodded. 'Yes, but we would rather keep that anonymous. Can you use another address? Perhaps his office in Prisght?'

Meg nodded again, spun the laptop around so that Rose could enter the address details, and then looked toward Sandy. 'Are you all on holiday? How did you find out about our dog and wedding ceremonies? We think it's beautiful that the bond between man and his best friend can be made even stronger.'

Sandy smiled, but Rose responded instead. 'I'm sorry, Meg; our Miss Truffa doesn't speak English. They don't teach it in Lovinkia. We'll be leaving on tomorrow's ferry. So can it be done that quickly?'

Nic nodded. 'I concur. Will you be ready by nine in the morning?'

Meg smiled. 'Yes, certainly. I'll let the resort people

know as they've already prepared a lovely scenic area. So, what is your dog's name?'

Nic grinned. 'Don't you mean my betrothed? His name is Joe Black.'

Meg laughed. 'Sorry, I hadn't done one of these marriages before,' and leaned towards him. 'And I don't think it's quite legal, but...' Nic waited for her to continue, however, the man from the tent had returned. 'I've completed the authorisation on your Credit Card, so we're ready to go whenever you are.'

Meg looked at him and smiled. 'We're on for tomorrow at nine, Mr Szertkovic.'

CHAPTER 4

In the morning, the group was lined up at the makeshift altar, and the two little dogs were dressed in tuxedos, including bow ties. Nic's outfit matched them exactly. Rose and Sandy were standing on either side of Nic, holding the leashes, and both wore white wedding dresses. The Celebrant was the same man from the tent, and there were about twenty well-dressed guests and thirty suitably dressed dogs. The music started, and the ceremony began, but suddenly, a couple interrupted the process, running toward the wedding group.

Rose noticed them. 'Damn, I guess my parents must have heard about it.' Her father looked at her sternly. 'Stop this at once. Just what are you doing here, Rosemary? Your brother rang to tell us you were getting married again.'

The Celebrant glared at them. 'Please sit down.' He then continued: 'We're gathered here to witness the union of this lovely couple...'

Rose sat down to address her parents: 'Hello, Father. Hello Mother. I'm not here to marry Nic. My

God, that would make me Rose Thorn, wouldn't it? I was, however, about to marry a sixty-five-year-old Dr Graham Garden up in Port Douglas, but fortunately, Nic saved me from being Rose Garden.'

Rose looked over at her mother as she started to swoon. Her father stood up and began again. 'What is this all about, Mr Thorn? And you too, Sandy? I am so disappointed you were also a part of it.'

Nic could see Sandy was about to unload on him, so he intervened. 'Now Zachariah and Jana, we are sorry you came all this way for a non-event. Rose is correct; there was to be a marriage. However, it was all part of an investigation into Social Security Fraud and Tax Evasion.'

The Celebrant looked at Nic with mouth agape, then looked over to his assistant and sat down, allowing Nic to continue. 'What you are doing is a fraud, whatever you view it. I'm here on behalf of the Brisbane Fraud Squad, and they'll meet with you to end all of this when you return from the island.'

Nic gathered himself and re-addressed her parents. 'Sorry, please forgive me. I assume you don't have anywhere to stay and I know a lovely suite that has just become available within this fine resort.'

Rose looked over to Nic. 'How would you be able to secure a room at such short notice?'

Nic smiled. 'It's all good. It's your room.'

Rose stared at him. 'No way, Nic. I'm not staying in a suite with my parents.'

Nic shook his head. 'Who said anything about that? We already have something new to investigate, which may be overseas this time, too. I'll leave the local police to sort it out from here, but in the meantime, we have to leave in a few hours to take a flight from Brisbane. I assume you are both interested in starting the next investigation?' Rose and Sandy nodded in agreement.

Nic then called over the concierge, arranged to transfer the booking to Rose's parents, and dropped a couple of hundred dollars onto the bar tab for the crowd and another hundred for the dogs. He then patted Budd and Yzah on the head and rang the owner to suggest a few days of recuperation on the island. She cheerfully accepted.

Within two hours, they were on the ferry heading back to Brisbane, and as they made their way down the aisle, Sandy noticed that two passengers had musical instrument cases on the seats next to them. 'Hey, we could have been in the posh seats at the front, but they said none were available, so unfortunately we'll have to sit next to Nic.'

They took their seats, and once underway, Rose started up about the recent capers they'd just finalised. 'So, the marriage scam stuff. What's it all about?'

Nic smiled. 'As I said, Social Security monitors marriage fraud, and sometimes there's a case for an investigation even when couples get married for the right reasons.'

'Has there ever been a case for someone to get married for the right reason?'

'Rose. Why are you so jaded? And yes, some people marry for love. I read that on the back of a door once. It was something like that or could have been in one of the many Beatles songs. Many of their songs had love in the title; 'Love me Do, She Loves You, All you need is Love''.

Nic suddenly broke into song, whispering the words in his best 'Liverpudlian' accent: 'Love, Love, Love...'

Rose looked at him. 'You can't pick winning lotto numbers, Nic.' He glanced at her and continued, albeit a little louder.

Rose sighed. 'Have you tried singing the second verse of the Australian National Anthem?' He looked at her again. 'All you need is Love, Love. Love is all you need.'

'Please don't do that.'

'What's that? Call you Love?'

'No, sing in a public place. We're on a ferry, you know.'

Suddenly, a deep voice was heard from the seat across the row as he began singing the second verse from the Beatles song. Rose was looking at the older man when another voice broke the silence. It was a woman's voice from somewhere else within the boat. Rose stood up from her seat and then looked down at Nic. 'See what you've started?'

A man standing next to the ferry attendant was

drinking a glass of water, donned a black plastic 'Beatle' wig, and took the microphone from her. Rose sat back down and shook her head. In the meantime, several people in the crowd were singing the chorus. '*Love, Love, Love.*'

Suddenly, a man and woman stood up front, and as they each had a trumpet started on the refrain at the start of the Beatles song. Rose looked over to Sandy and Nic, as they had joined in with the singing, this time out aloud with everyone else: 'Damn you, John, Paul, George and Ringo.'

The song went through a few more verses, and finally, the ferry driver requested the passengers lower the noise as he was finding it hard to concentrate. All the passengers clapped, and when the ferry arrived at Redcliffe, Nic went up to the trumpeter and shook his hand.

Rose had stopped to wait for him to return. 'You set this all up, didn't you? I think I know that guy from somewhere.'

Nic shook his head. 'He's one of the greatest Australian Jazz artists. It was James and one of his mates. They'd been holidaying on the other side of the island.'

Sandy laughed. 'So, you did set it up then? I heard that his trumpet is worth about a hundred thousand dollars. It's made of platinum.'

Nic nodded. 'Yep, I've heard that too, and I also know there's a Beatles convention in Brisbane this week and that some of them had been on the island, but other than that, this is what people sometimes do, randomly break into song. I once saw it in a movie; who knew it worked in real life?'

They collected their luggage and went to the car. The 'Beatles crowd' had boarded a bus emblazoned with the 'Magical Mystery Tour' graphics, and they were still singing. Meantime, James M and his entourage climbed into a waiting limousine.

Nic dropped Sandy and Rose at their West End home, where Dog awaited their arrival. It was wailing as if he hadn't been fed for hours. Nic helped them with the luggage and looked down at the cat. 'I thought you told Dave next door looks after Dog whilst you're both away.'

Sandy nodded. 'He does, Nic. It's just after six thirty now, so Dog wants an after-dinner snack.'

'When did Dave last feed him?'

Rose smiled. 'At six.'

Nic laughed. 'See you guys back at the airport in a couple of days then, and we'll head off to a lovely island renowned for its lush greenery, sparkling mountains, cascading waterfalls, and enchanting atmosphere. It's one of the best islands in the world.' He saluted, stepped back into the car, and headed home himself.

Rose and Sandy relocated to their rear deck and were sipping on Chardonnay whilst Dog was looking for his pre-bed-time snack. 'So this thing with Nic?

Are you still OK with it? We've only known him about six months.'

Sandy nodded. 'Yes, it's weird. We can trust him to keep us safe, and that's what matters, right?'

Rose did some internet searching on the Quantum Palladium Credit Card. 'Hey, there's no such thing as a Quantum Card, so that card Nic gave the guy at the tent must have been bogus. How did he manage to get it authorised?'

Sandy looked at her. 'Perhaps it was a scam?' Rose continued. 'But you can't scam a scammer. It can't be within the rules.'

Sandy did some searching of her own. 'You know there's nothing on Nic Thorn either, so I just searched 'Nicllaus Szertkovic', and there's a whole website about him. It says he's holidaying in Australia with his two dogs and his two wives, Rosandali and Sanzha.'

Rose pulled up the website and then rang Nic. It went to voicemail: 'Hello, you have reached Nicllaus's phone. Please leave a message.'

Rose commented despairingly: 'Damn you, Nic.'

CHAPTER 5

A couple of days later, Rose and Sandy were in the Brisbane Airport waiting for Nic to arrive. He was right on time but only had a barrel bag, whilst they had two suitcases each. Rose was the first to notice: 'OK, Nic. Overseas, you said, exotic, so where is it? Hawaii? The Bahamas? The Maldives?'

Nic shrugged, handed over their tickets, and they read them: 'Tasmania is not overseas, and we're sitting together in a row and not in Business Class. I call dibs for the window.'

'I call dibs for the aisle then, and you, Nic, will be in the middle.'

'Ah, the rose. I'll be between a thorn and a rose.....mm, that doesn't work? Can you do me a favour? Please go through your suitcases and divvy them; you only take one each. I'll get the QANTAS Lounge to take care of the cases left behind, and we'll pick them up when we return.'

They grumbled a bit more about being in cattle class and not having the right outfits, so he led them to the QANTAS Lounge, where they fed on tapas and sipped champagne.

Sandy took up her grievances once again when they were on the plane. 'Do you know how cold it is this time of year in Tasmania?'

'Boy, you never give up, do you? I'm sorry, I said overseas '*maybe*', but first, we have this one to deal with. Something is going on in Tasmania that I have been asked to look into. The long-extinct Tasmanian Tiger, also known as a Thylacine, has made a come-back, and some guy is running wilderness tours looking for it.'

Rose shook her head. 'You mean we are going down there to look for the Tasmanian tiger? Wasn't the last one seen in the 1930s in a Hobart Zoo? Cripes, it's a long way to go to look for something that doesn't exist.'

'Good point, Rose. Well, your brother lives in Claremont, and he's near the famous Cadbury factory. You've always said when in doubt, go to chocolate.'

'I haven't spoken to him for months, and he won't even know we are coming. It might scare the bee-geezers out of him.'

Sandy interjected. 'Sorry, Rose. When I spoke to him the other day, I did mention that you might be a runaway bride. He said we'd be welcome anytime.'

Rose shrugged. 'I guess that's how my folks heard about the wedding then.'

Sandy nodded. 'So Nic, do we get names like Rosie

Rhynge and Sandra Olsson, as we used in the Adelaide caper? Or do we go there pretending to be Nancy Drew and Miss Marple?'

'Nope. You're just Rose Palmer and Sandy Fraser, but there will be safari suits, so start practising your best Steve Irwin's 'Crikey' as we'll be representing the Tasmanian Parks and Wildlife Service.'

'Don't you ever get sick of being someone else?'

'Nope, but I can easily get hold of credit cards with other names for you. I am considering using 'Daisy' and 'Daffy'. How do you like those names?'

'Nope. Rose Palmer and Sandy Fraser will be good, thanks.'

He handed them the credit cards, and Rose looked at them. 'I was expecting Quantum Palladium Cards. What are these?'

Nic smiled. 'So, you noticed that?' Rose continued. 'I googled Quantum. There's no such Card company on the internet. Are you pulling a scam yourself?'

Nic lowered his voice. 'Well, Rose, in my line of business, we have to allow for all contingencies. In the case of that card, when the store rings up for authorisation, it will be approved, but the actual 'sale' doesn't go through as it flags at the Bank Card Authorisation Centre that the transaction involves a suspect merchant. I don't often use it.'

Nic pulled the card from his wallet and showed it to her. Rose noticed the card had no name, only the sixteen-digit account number. 'There's no name on this card either.'

Nic nodded. 'Yep, so I can use whatever name I like.' He then handed over the two other cards to them. 'Use these cards as often as you like.'

Sandy nodded. 'I wish you had given them to us earlier. We needed these in the airport to buy things for this trip, like woollen thermals and girlie stuff.'

'Didn't you pack those already? You only have one suitcase each?'

Sandy smiled. 'Well, we did, but nothing wears better than the thermals you buy at the Merino store at Brisbane airport, which is what the shop assistant told us.'

Nic ignored the comment. 'OK, I'm going to sleep now, so wake me when we get there, will you? By the way, I'm a light sleeper, so don't search through any of my manly stuff. Flight time is just under three hours.'

Nic went off to sleep and was woken by the weight of the women's heads resting on each of his shoulders about an hour later. They were both asleep, and he couldn't move his arms as they were pinned against his side. A flight attendant came past, looked at him, and stifled a laugh. 'Can I get you something, sir? Like another cup of chai tea and a long straw?'

'No, but thank you. How about you ask the pilot to roll the plane side to side to wake these two sleeping beauties up? Nothing too scary, just a little bit of a wobble.'

'Certainly, sir, I will see what I can do.'

The flight attendant went up to the intercom and asked the passengers to return to their seats in preparation for landing, then looked at Nic. 'I must apologise to our guest seated in Seat 14B, it is not our policy to wobble the plane to wake any sleeping passengers.'

Sandy and Rose were now awake and re-started the conversation trying to rile Nic. Rose managed a stretch in the shared space and leaned forward. 'OK, I get The Beatles wanting love, love, love, but marriage is not for me, never, never, never again.'

'You're still so young, Rose; I hope you keep your hope chest stocked just in case. What about you, Sandy?'

'Me either.'

Nic shook his head. 'Cripes, you guys and your histories. I get it, but it's water under the bridge, as sometimes you jump into the water, get cold feet, and jump out straight away. But there are also those times that you jump in, roll onto your back, and float along wherever the river takes you.'

Sandy leaned forward to talk across Nic. 'Is he always like this?'

'I think so. I have only known him about five hours more than you. He may just be overdosing on his happy pills again.'

They disembarked and met Rose's brother in the waiting area. He held out his hand to Nic. 'Arnie Palmer.' Nic collected the luggage from the carousel.

'Nic Thorn, nice to meet you, Arnie,' shook his hand and whispered to Rose, 'Your brother is Arnold Palmer? I assume he plays golf?'

'Yes, he does, but why? Do you already know an Arnold Palmer?'

'Yep, he was a USA Champion Golfer in the early sixties. I think he won almost a hundred championships and died two years ago.'

'I might have heard of him, but please don't mention it.'

Arnie led them to the car park and pointed out his car, it was a sporty two-door Nissan 300Z. Nic looked at it, then at all their luggage. 'Sorry, Arnie, it's a nice buggy, but we'll be doing a bit of bush bashing while we are here, so I've arranged the transport. If you'd take Rose now, that's fine. I'll take the luggage and meet you at your place.'

Sandy grinned at Nic's comment about the car. 'What car did you get us this time? A Mercedes-Benz? One of those spacey, spaced out, spacey things or just a Mini-Minor with ambition?'

'It's a Land Cruiser Troopy. It's nothing fancy, but it might do the trick.'

About forty minutes later, Nic parked the Troopy outside Arnie's place, and they had to wait for the others to arrive.

Arnie and Rose eventually arrived, stopped the Nissan in the driveway and Arnie noticed Nic and

Sandy had already arrived. 'When did you tell Nic where I lived?'

'I didn't. That's just what he does. He knows, finds, buys, sells, and does stuff. Sorry, we probably won't need to stay here either. Nic probably has us staying somewhere five stars.'

'By the way, Eva and I have a trial separation, and she has taken little Emme with her, too.'

Rose looked over to him. 'I didn't know; I'm so sorry. Any chance of, you know, coming full circle and you guys working things out?'

'I don't know. I think she wants a hero. I don't know what to think. Tell me about Nic. Is he the right one for you?'

Rose nodded. 'Well, if you can recall, at Uncle Albert's funeral about two months ago, I needed a '+1', someone like a mild-mannered 'Clark Kent', but Nic turned up. He isn't exactly the Vita Brevis dating site regular, and he even wore an Armani suit to the funeral. I mean, who does that?'

Rose noticed Sandy and Nic had not yet moved towards them, so she continued: 'As for what it is between Nic and me, I don't know Arnie, but it has been a great ride with Sandy by my side and Nic beside us. Neither Sandy nor I want to get off the Nic Thorn merry-go-round anytime soon.'

Rose opened the door and stepped out. 'Just catching up. It's been a while, and he just told me Eva and Emme had moved out.'

Nic nodded. 'Sorry to hear, Arnie. We don't start our thing for a few days. See if you can take a couple of days off, and let's have a round of golf tomorrow; after that, do you think you would be available to be our driver around Tasmania?'

Arnie smiled. 'Yes, sure, Nic. I have some holiday leave to take anyway, and the Boag's Brewery can do without me for a day or two. I've told my boss I'm not taking my trial separation well, so he'll understand. Where will we be driving to?'

Nic nodded. 'Over to the East Coast first, to the Wineglass Bay area. We're booked into the Freycinet Lodge for a couple of days. I'll make a call so you can stay there too if you like, then we'll drive over to the west coast, up near the town of Burnie.'

Arnie smiled. 'I'll pay my way if that's OK.' He whispered to Rose. 'Do you think he can talk to Eva? I miss her and Emme terribly.'

Rose nodded. 'Tell you what, Arnie, if you want to get back with her, and I know you do, it will be all of us, not just Nic, that will help you out.'

'Thanks, Rose. So, see you all in the morning then. I'll set up a tee-off time of eleven a.m. Nic and I will play nine holes. Will you and Sandy drive the golf carts?' Rose nodded again. 'Sure. Sounds like a plan.'

Nic looked back to Arnie. 'Tell you what, if I win, I'll pay for your stay at Freycinet. If I lose, you take me to the Hobart Casino for a couple of hours.'

'You're on.'

It was 11 a.m. and the group was standing at the first tee at the Claremont Golf Club. Nic had hired clubs, and Arnie provided the tees and golf balls. Rose and Sandy wore suitably bold golf attire, all clashing checks and stripes having recently been purchased from the Pro Shop. Nic was dressed like a professional golfer in the latest branded golf wear, also recently purchased from the Pro Shop. Arnie was dressed in a collar-less T-shirt and long basketball shorts. Rose and Arnie were in one cart, whilst Nic and Sandy were in the other, waiting their turn to tee off.

Rose climbed out of her cart and ambled over to Nic. 'Have you played before? I assume you know that Eva was part of the Australian Ladies Professional Golf circuit, and Arnie is also quite handy around the greens. I think he plays off scratch. They used to play a lot together before having Emme.'

'Yep, I know she's a champion golfer, and he would be pretty good too.'

'So, what's this all about then? Eva had to step back from golf when they had Emme, and Arnie sounds like he's got a little lost not having them around.'

'Rose, it's about courage and confidence, which you two Palmers kids seem to have lost somewhere. I've played before, but it's been a while. Golf is just a nice walk spoilt by trying to hit a horrid little white ball into a horrid little hole with a horrid little stick. Easy.'

It was finally their turn. They watched as the group

in front moved off and were out of driving range. 'So, what do you drive, Nic? Around two hundred to two fifty metres?'

'Something like that, Arnie. My honours, I assume?' Nic strode up to the grassy block, pushed his tee into the ground, placed the ball atop, took a few practice swings, addressed the ball, and commenced his full swing, but just as he reached the apex of his back-swing, Sandy's phone rang, so he miss-timed the follow through. The ball skewed across the grass, landing short of the ladies' tee, stopping twenty-five metres in front.

'Nic, I call a mulligan. Sandys's phone rang in the middle of your swing.'

'Thanks, Arnie.'

They all looked over to Sandy as she had moved away to take the call, but they could still overhear that she was very annoyed. 'Leave me alone. Yes, I am Sandra Fraser from Hill End Terrace, Brisbane. No, I don't have a loan with Community Bank. I don't even have an account there, so go away.'

Sandy disconnected, and Nic went over to her. 'Sandy, what's up? And thanks, as I was, it would never be a good drive anyway. I didn't have my lucky Tam O'Shanter or my fancy plus fours on my head.'

Sandy sighed heavily. 'I have been getting these calls for the last couple of weeks, and they're leaving angry messages, too. Some Collection Agency from Brisbane says they're about to take recovery action because I haven't been making any loan payments for months. I don't have a loan, and they say they've been sending mail, but I haven't received any. I don't know what it's all about and don't know what to do.'

Nic nodded. 'Leave it with me, Sandy. I'll make a call and get you a new number. The last two numbers will be reversed to make it easy to remember. Please turn your phone off, and let's get this underway.'

Arnie was watching Nic ready himself on the tee block. 'Hey, Rose.'

'Yes, Arnie'

'He does that sort of thing, too?'

'Yep, our Mr Nic Thorn is a man of many talents. He does stuff, finds stuff, and forgets stuff too. Sandy told him to get stuffed once, and he shouted at us on this trip to Tasmania. He's also met Father and Mother and my ex, Michael, and that was interesting, to say the least.'

'What else does he do? I mean, does he kill people?'

'Oh no, Arnie, nothing like that, although he gently reminds them of the need for good manners. He doesn't carry a gun either, and it's not his style.'

Nic re-addressed the ball and smacked it straight down the middle; it bounced off to the left, then bounced high when it hit a cement cart path that added another fifty metres to the drive. It then rolled back onto the middle of the fairway and landed just short of the group that had played off in front of Nic and Arnie. The group leader turned around to remind

Nic pleasantly that he should have waited a little longer before teeing off.

'That's about a three hundred and twenty metres drive. Good show, old man.'

'Drive for show and putt for dough, they say, Arnie.'

Arnie hit his golf ball up the middle; they finished the hole, and Nic's phone rang. 'Yep, good, done. Thanks.' Nic turned to Sandy. 'You now have a new number. Also, my people have told me that there is a record of you having a loan with the Community Bank in Brisbane. It was taken out about five months ago. My guys also contacted the Collections Agency and reminded them of the Banking Code regarding pursuing debts. The Agency agreed to meet with you thirty days back in Brisbane. I will be attending as your Financial Counsellor.'

'Rose.'

'Yes, Arnie'

Is he 'Bruce' Wayne, Batman, or both of them simultaneously?'

'I don't know, but he does like wearing disguises. I don't think he's a superhero, but I can't say for sure as I haven't seen him in his underwear or wearing a cape.'

Their phones didn't ring again, and by the time the group had reached the 6th hole, Nic had decided he'd had enough of golf. 'I have other things to do, Arnie, so may I concede?'

'Sure. So, it was two hours you wanted at the

Casino? I will set it up, and how about we have dinner there tonight? It is on me.'

'On one condition, though.'

'What's that?'

'You bring your wife Eva and Emme along. I'm sure Rose would like to catch up with them.'

'I think she would be OK with that.'

The group turned the carts around and returned to the clubrooms for lunch. Whilst they were having lunch, the Club Captain came over to their table and introduced himself, then gently reminded Nic that the group in front must always be out of driving range. He then nodded towards Rose and Sandy.

'Nice outfits, but please don't wear such bold attire here again as it scares the wildlife, and Wilbur, it's good to see you back here too. Please see if your lovely wife Eva can come back to play for us. It's been a while... our 1st Pennants Team miss her, and so do we.'

Nic leaned over to Rose and whispered. 'Wilbur? Arnie's name is Wilbur. No wonder he uses Arnie.'

'Yes, it is. Full name, 'Wilbur Arnold Jefferson Palmer,' but I assumed you knew that.'

Nic shook his head. 'No, Rose, I didn't. I must be slipping. Maybe I've been out in the sun too long playing golf.'

They finished their meal and returned to Arnie's place to discuss searching for the elusive Tiger. 'Nic, you know that the recent Thylacine sightings have been nowhere near the east coast. It's over on the west coast, up near the town of Corinna.'

'Yep, I do.'

'Besides that, Eva and I spent our honeymoon at Freycinet Lodge. Has it been five years already, Rose?'

Rose smiled. 'I think he knows that to Arnie,' whilst looking at Nic. 'Our Nic knows other stuff too. Just act surprised if Eva and Emme happen to turn up at Freycinet for the weekend.'

Nic whispered. 'You already know me too well, Rose.'

Arnie nodded. 'We do need a weekend away, and Eva has been nagging me to take her back.' He returned from his office with a large fold-out map of Tasmania, scanned his fingers across the page and looked up. 'It's about a six-hour drive across and up the middle through Campbelltown, over to Burnie, and then the Murch highway. We should be there late afternoon if we leave early in the morning. I can give a guy call, and we could stay at the nearest Great Western.'

'Is that five stars?'

'Nope, I don't think so. It might be three.'

'When Rose and I stay away from home, we only stay four-star minimum. Don't we, Nic?'

'That they do, Arnie, and don't worry about the accommodation. I've already arranged it as there's a place called 'The Tarkine Hotel' that might suit them instead. There's a wildlife refuge place there, too. Maybe we can meet some of the local fluffy critters up close up now, like wombats, devils, wallabies, and maybe an extinct Tasmanian Tiger or two.'

Arnie folded up the map, Nic cleared away the plates, and they moved outside to return to the Hotel. Sandy and Rose got into the car, and Nic approached Arnie. They exchanged a few words, and Nic climbed into the car and drove away.

Rose looked at him. 'What did you say to him?'

'Secret men's business, Rose.'

The group arrived back at Hobart's Wrest Point Casino around 3 p.m., so they walked around old Hobart Town, looking at Salamanca Markets and the waterfront. A Maxi Yacht was moored in the harbour. 'That's a tough challenge, even for a He-Man like me, who might also be Batman.'

'Don't tell us you have done a Sydney to Hobart yacht race?'

'Nope, not one, but two. One is on a Maxi like that, and the other is on a twenty-five-footer. That's exciting; it took four days and almost killed me.'

They walked around the wharf area, collected a few souvenirs, and then returned to the Casino Hotel bar for pre-dinner drinks. Nic leaned toward them. 'I've asked Arnie to wear a suit at dinner, so can you guys find something nice to wear too? Use the Credit cards as needed, and I'll see you back at The Point Restaurant at seven.'

They watched him walk away, and Sandy whispered:

'Did you hear that? Nic just permitted us to go shopping.'

Rose was still looking at Nic. 'Yes, I heard that too, but he also asked Arnie to wear a suit, and that's what I'm perturbed about. Just what is Nic up to?'

Rose picked out a moss green cashmere jumper worn with designer jeans, and Sandy found a locally made dress. Matching handbags and shoes were considered, but they both felt guilty about spending over four hundred dollars on their outfits.

They were now waiting outside the restaurant for Nic and Arnie. Eva and Emme had already gone past and had taken their seats inside. The lift chimed, and two well-dressed gentlemen stepped out in dark grey Armani suits and matching trilbies. Sandy and Rose saw them at the same time. 'Nice'.

Arnie walked up to Rose, kissed her on both cheeks and held out his hand. 'Good evening, Rosemary Palmer. My name is Jefferson Palmer, and I'm pleased to make your acquaintance.'

'Is that you under the Armani, Arnie? I mean, like, wow.'

'Your friend, Nic Thorn, reminded me that I'm married to one of the most talented golfers and beautiful women here in Hobart, probably the whole of Tasmania. I can continue to be Arnie Palmer, the golfer and Accounts Clerk at Boags or Jefferson Palmer, my child's mother, deserves to be with.'

Rose smiled. 'Touché, Nic.'

The four entered the restaurant, and one of the wait staff hurried up to them, 'Your other guests have already arrived. Please follow me to your seats.' Nic led the way, and as they neared the table, Eva looked up, but she only had eyes for Arnie in the Armani suit. Sandy, Rose, and Nic stepped out of the way so he could take centre stage: 'Good evening, Mrs Eva Palmer; my name is Jefferson Palmer. I will be your date tonight and, if all goes well, your partner for the rest of our lives.'

Eva could only manage 'Wow' and she looked over to Emme, who was busy with a pencil and colouring in the book. 'Daddy's here. Would you like to say hello?'

The little girl looked at her father and smiled. 'You took your fuzz off your face, Daddy. Mummy had said that you didn't want to. I didn't like it either, but now you did just for me.' She climbed down from the chair and hugged him around the waist.

'This is the new me, Eva. I'm sorry I took us for granted, and I ask that you put it all behind us. You and I can roll over onto our backs and float along the river hand in hand, wherever it takes us.'

Rose leaned into Nic. 'You recycled that quote for him, and thanks for all this.'

'My pleasure. So, let's eat, then tomorrow we'll drive over to Freycinet, and the next day we will don the safari suits to hunt for a Tasmanian tiger. Crikey.'

Eva looked up. 'Oh, Jeff, or is it Jefferson? Anyway, I won a weekend away at Freycinet Lodge, too, but only for this weekend. Funny, though, I don't recall entering any competitions. Do you mind if we tag along?'

Jefferson smiled. 'It will only ever be Jefferson, and you are both most welcome.'

The meals were served, and Rose noticed it was nearing eleven, so she decided to call it a night and leaned toward Nic.

'Thanks, as sometimes we all need a reminder of what's important, don't we?'

CHAPTER 6

In the morning, they met at Jefferson's place, climbed into the Troopy, waved to Eva and Emme, and drove east towards Freycinet Lodge. 'Why are we off to Freycinet? It is completely the wrong direction.'

'Rose, not everything has to be about everything. Sometimes it's good to do something for nothing, to see if something becomes something.'

Jefferson looked at him. 'Explain that again, Nic.'

'Well, the thing is, you don't know me, and you haven't seen your sister for five years. We've just asked you to drive across Tasmania in a car you don't know, leaving a wife and child at home that you don't want to leave, and you are asking me to explain things?'

'Good point. So, it's all a test and depends on how I go, and I guess you'll have to decide that I can keep driving, or you drop me off somewhere in the Midlands to make my way home?'

'Nic wouldn't do that. He will at least give you pocket money to catch the bus.'

'Thanks, Rose.' Sandy updated him about Brisbane. 'We had to close the shop when the new road was built at Brett's Wharf. I think that's what started the downhill spiral for Uncle Albert.'

Jefferson responded. ''The She Shed', guys, I always thought it was an excellent name for a dress shop. What happened in the end? Did you manage to sell the business? Did Uncle Albert help you out?'

'Nope, we just closed it. The building was demolished, and Albert got next to nothing from the Government, just enough to payout the mortgage and business debts. The rest went to keeping him comfortable at the Royal Brisbane Hospital until he passed. The funeral was a blast. It was held at the Marriott Hotel, and the room was done up as a Bedouin Tent. Some bizarre Uncle Albert references to people being 'too-tense.''

'What about the will reading? Nothing left to divvy up?'

Rose updated things now. 'Nope. He had no money left; the Brett Whitely Painting, Big Blue Lavender Bay, the one that Father had in his study? It's been confirmed as a genuine fake, and Michael even made a scene about being left out of the will. There was nothing left.'

'Tell me more about Michael then. Is he still with Dimond, and how are his kids, Lucy and Skye? Those names still crack me up. Surely, they knew of the Beatles' song; Lucy in the Sky with Diamonds?'

'I didn't know that either. Nic had to tell me.'

'But Rose, you don't like music from beyond the fifties, and you confuse Ed Sheeran with Prince Harry?'

'Yes, she does', Nic responded, then added. 'I mean, they are both red-heads, both got married recently, both English and I bet they sing while sitting on the throne, although one is a toilet and the other a big red wooden chair.'

Nic and Jefferson started laughing.

'Hey, that's not funny, guys.'

'Yes, it is Rose,' came from Jefferson, 'And tell me, why does Nic sometimes call you Miss Panda-Eyes? What's the story behind that? Hang on. I'll pull in here for petrol, a quick bite, and a coffee if that's OK.'

They agreed, and whilst eating their snacks, Sandy pulled the link up on the net. It was a clear vision of Rose doing pirouettes along a waterfall within an exhibition at the Gallery of Modern Art in Brisbane. The final view focused on her face and two very black circles of running mascara. Nic tried his best not to laugh at the vision. 'And that is why our Rose is sometimes called 'Miss Panda-Eyes.'

Rose grimaced. 'The things we do....'

They arrived at Freycinet Lodge and saw Eva and Emme were already there, having driven in the Nissan. Eva was beaming when they arrived, and Jefferson approached, kissing them both.

'Don't ever get rid of this car, Jefferson. I understand why Arnie wouldn't let me drive it, but it suits Jefferson in spades. He won't have any trouble letting me drive either because that's the type of man he is. He shares things with his wife, including his little sports car.'

Emme looked up to her Father. 'Mummy got caught speeding. She told me not to tell you, but I can't keep a secret. Sorry Mummy.'

Jefferson looked at her. 'How fast were you going?' Eva looked at him. 'Well, I thought the cruise control set on a hundred and ten, but it was a hundred and twenty. When I got out of the car, the policeman looked me over, and after I explained to him what I'd done, he let me off with a warning.'

'Nic, didn't I tell you she was the most beautiful woman in the whole of Tasmania? I think we are going to have to move beyond these shores. Look out; main-land, the Palmers are coming over.'

Nic nodded. 'Leave that one with me, Jefferson.'

They checked in at the Reservations Desk and agreed to meet a couple of hours later for dinner after doing some exploring of their own. Sandy and Rose offered to take Emme for the afternoon to give quality time to the recently re-acquainted couple.

It was now after 7:30 p.m., and Eva and Jefferson were yet to arrive, so Rose moved away from the table, called his mobile, and returned. 'They are busy guys, um, apparently, they haven't seen each other for a while and want to catch up, and they have asked me if we could take Emme for a sleepover with us. I hope that's OK, Sandy. They have left an overnight bag at the Front Desk for Emme.'

Emme squirmed. 'Are Mummy and Daddy coming to dinner, Aunty Rosie?'

'No, sorry, little one, they are busy tonight looking for something special for you in the forest. Daddy is coming with us for a few days to help us look for a Tasmanian tiger. Would that be OK with you?'

Emme nodded. 'Mummy and I are moving back home whilst he is away. Don't tell him, as it's a secret.'

In the morning, seated at breakfast, Jefferson and Eva behaved like newlyweds, so Rose politely reminded them they were in public when Nic walked up. 'There's been a change of plans. It looks like we have to move today to Corinna by this afternoon. I've been told there's a big bus of Eco-tourists on their way down from Launceston, and the Forestry guys are worried about what forty trampling hikers will do to pristine forest, so they want us there ASAP to look. The tourist groups are always better in lower numbers, so the forest damage is minimised. A large group is too much for the local site to handle. Will that be OK with everyone?'

Eva nodded. 'All good from Emme and me. We can return this morning, and I can't wait to get back into the Nissan and scream down the highway, but what about the rooms? Surely, we can't walk out. What happens to the booking?'

'I can take care of that too. So, are we all good to go?'

'Yes, give us an hour to pack up, and we'll meet back in the car park at ten.'

They were waiting for Jefferson, and finally, he came out holding Eva's hand on one side and Emme's on the other. Nic looked at him. 'You don't have to do this, Jefferson. Take your wife and child and return to Hobart if you like. There is no need to drive for us.'

'Nope, I can't do that. Maybe Arnie would back down, but Jefferson is a man of his word and will stay until the end. I am in. Eva and Emme are on board, too. Let's get this show on the road.' He approached Eva, kissed her on the top of her head, hugged Emme, and then saluted Nic.

'What are you guys waiting for? Get in the Troopy.'

Rose leaned forward as they were making their way back to the highway. 'Hey Nic, the car driver in Adelaide, we called him 'Driver'. So should we be calling Jefferson that, too? All part of your secret stuff we've signed up for?'

'Good idea, Rose. Please don't mention that he lives in Hobart or is related to you. You do look alike, but he doesn't have your retrousse nose. We can work on a backstory between now and Burnie. It has to be convincing, nothing clever, and just very ordinary. That's all part of the Society of the Secret Squirrel and keeping your acorn seeds hidden in plain sight.'

Rose called out from the back. 'So, we can't call him 'Bruce' Wayne or 'Bruce' Banner then?'

Nic nodded. 'Nope, but 'Bruce' is a good name; there is no need for a surname. What's the back story then?'

Jefferson looked over to Nic. 'Make it golf. I can play, and we can talk about the courses around Adelaide, Hobart, and Brisbane.'

'Yep, I can work with that. I've played some USA courses, including Firestone and Torrey Pines.'

Jefferson chortled. 'Those are two of the courses from Microsoft Golf. No wonder you knew what a 'mulligan' was the other day at the tee block.'

Nic was a little taken aback. 'You mean it's not a real golf term?'

'Nope.'

'So, I have got one up on the great Nic Thorn? Maybe you have to call me Great Sensei then?'

'Not yet, gakusei. So, let's stick with 'Bruce' from Brisbane.'

Rose nodded. 'That was easy. What do we need to work on next, Nic? Secret handshakes?'

Nic smiled. 'Maybe, but the back story might need more work. There are portfolios on the seat there. It will give you some insight into the history of the Thylacine and the background of their habitat. Also, the environment around Corinna, and the likelihood that this is not a large scam.'

Sandy called out. 'So what way are we playing? Is

it a scam or a legitimate wildlife professional with a genuine personal agenda to find and save the Tasmanian tiger?

'That's the thing, guys, I don't know yet, and 'Bruce', I need you not to know anything. You are our driver and don't know what we're doing here. Sandy and Rose, you're working for me as Research Assistants on a Field Scholarship from the University of Queensland, as they won't check that. I will be Dr Nickolas Brown, a Veterinarian and Thylacine expert from Sydney. Anyone who checks will find a LinkedIn profile, a brief history at the Australian National University in Canberra, and that I have been studying Sumatran Tigers abroad.'

Nic stopped the conversation as his phone pinged. 'I have to make a private call, Jefferson. Can we make another stop for petrol and coffee?'

Jefferson turned off the highway and pulled the car over at the service station, where they stocked up with food. 'The nearest town is Penguin. It's ten minutes away, but I can take this exit.'

They arrived in Penguin, and Nic stepped out to make the call, so Jefferson turned to face Rose. 'So, what was the secret all about?'

Rose piped up from the back seat. 'It could have been the Prime Minister, as far we know. Nic walks off to take all his calls. It's all part of his secret stuff. He does stuff, says stuff, and keeps stuff secret.'

Nic returned and had overheard the comment.

'Well, you'll all know soon enough. A couple of things have come up as part of the investigation. We'll have to stop at the airport in Burnie as I have to take a short trip to King Island.'

Jefferson looked over at him. 'We can't drive there as they haven't finished building the bridge yet. It's about two hundred kilometres from Tassie. A long swim.'

Nic waggled his finger at them. 'Yep. That's the other thing; I'll be flying courtesy of my finger. I'm clever like that.'

They arrived at Burnie and drove to the airport. Nic pointed out the Sharp Airlines plane. 'See, my finger knows all and sees all. It is the index to everything.'

Rose looked at the size of the little aeroplane, then back to Nic. 'Err, there's something else I didn't put on my Vita Brevis dating app. I don't like flying.'

'I've only booked one seat anyway. The plane was full.'

Nic organised his flight ticket, and they went into the café. 'It's about a thirty-minute flight, then I have to have a word to some people about certain people making my people a little less people-friendly, and I'll be back here by four to restart our trip. Although we might have to stay here in Burnie if things change.'

'*Sharp Flight to King Island is now boarding. Please move to Gate 2.*'

Sandy nodded. 'That's great, but what will we do for four hours?'

Nic smiled. 'Go nuts.'

Jefferson nodded. 'Yep, will do. It's about an hour away.'

Rose looked at him. 'I'm for it. I've never been there. It takes about an hour to climb, so that will work.'

The group waited for Nic to lift off and returned to the car. Sandy looked at both of them. 'I have no idea what you are talking about, but I'm for it too.'

Rose sat in the front. 'We're going nuts for Stanley.'

Sandy piped up. 'Who's Stanley?'

'It's where the nut is.'

Sandy shook her head. 'Is this a bit like who's on first?'

'Not at all. Stanley is the town's name, and the nut is a hill you climb to take in the view and meet some penguins.'

'Oh, I'm glad that's solved then. The next issue is, did either of you find out why Nic went to King Island?'

Jefferson and Rose shook their heads. 'Nope.'

They headed to Stanley and returned to Burnie air- port around 4 p.m. to collect Nic. He ambled up to them. 'I had to meet and greet the local Detectives investigating this Tiger thing. They confirmed that a trio is involved, and they've been setting things up on King Island. About nine months ago, they stepped up their operations by getting access to a puppy farm in Burnie. Anyhow, let's talk about something else to lighten the mood.'

Sandy started reading from her phone about the history of Burnie. 'Hey, did you know this place is named after those two guys on Sesame Street, Bert and Ernie? When they merged the names, they called it Bernie.'

Rose looked at her. 'What site are you looking at?'

'Wickie-peedia Tasmania. I think it's a homage to the Australian guy that the Americans are trying to catch up with. He was born in Tasmania.'

Jefferson laughed, and then Rose called over to Nic. 'So, are you planning to leave us and go off yourself again? There is no 'I' in team, you know.'

Nic nodded. 'Yep, sorry about that. I've spent a long time working independently and got caught up in the stuff. Next time, I'll drag you into the stuff once it gets exciting.'

Sandy called out. 'Is there anything else you need to tell us about this little soirée you've lined up?'

'Well, there's something else you need to know. It's just under two hours to go, and we'll be in Corinna. Keep working on your background stories and keeping them simple. Remember that he is 'Bruce', I am Dr Nickolas Brown, and you two are doped out Uni students.'

Rose interjected. 'Hey, that's not fair. I didn't do drugs in Uni. I was busy getting married to Michael at nineteen, and 'Bruce', you didn't even come to my wedding.'

'Yes, I did.'

'You did, but 'Bruce' didn't. Remember that.'

Jefferson continued: 'OK, then, Dr Nickolas Brown, tell me about the timing of this again. We're about two hours out, and you've said that the Eco tourist bus left Launceston this morning. By my reckoning, we will arrive around four, so the tourist bus could have already left Corinna. They'd only be there for the day. 'Day-trippers, day-trippers, yeah, it took me so long to find out, and I found out."

'Beatles fan then, Bruce?'

'Yep.'

Nic nodded. 'Good, I'll use that. Rose and I used a safe word in Brisbane during the Art Gallery caper in case something went awry. This time, we will use 'beetles,' It means that if any of us uses the word beetles, or if we hear the word beetles, we walk away. The cover is blown. Got it, guys?'

Rose nodded. 'So, what is the ploy then? They'll be gone before we get there?'

'Nope, as the driver must complete his driving log before he leaves, mandatory breaks, and all that. If that fails, then the bus has been having engine trouble. He might delay the return trip until we arrive.'

'Is the bus driver one of your guys?'

'He's not on my payroll, but I have his Bank Account details if he ensures the bus hasn't left. I'll need to scope out a few things before the bus leaves, so I'll drop a couple of dollars in the account if he stays in town.'

The group went quiet for the rest of the trip, and around 4 p.m., they finally arrived. The Launceston tourist bus was still parked on the main street, and the back engine flap was up. Nic knew the driver had to make the second ploy regarding the delayed return, so he had Jefferson slow down to chat with the bus driver. 'All good here, mate?'

'Yes, thank you. I'm giving it a few minutes before the drive back to Lonnie. The passengers have boarded, and the guide is winding things up inside.'

Nic nodded. 'Did anything happen during their hike?'

'Nope, we arrived here just before eleven. I'd fed them on the bus, then dropped them off at the animal refuge pens to look at the animals. They made the two-hour hike in, an hour search for the tiger, and a hours walk out. I picked them up again at four.'

Nic signalled to 'Bruce' to park, and they all climbed out of the Troopy. 'Remember, guys, I am Dr Nickolas Brown, the Thylacine expert. I am going on the bus to get the guide and bring him out; then, the bus will leave. We are in play, so be careful. We don't know what this is yet, and remember, don't get your photo taken by the people on the bus.'

Nic climbed onto the bus. There was a round of applause, and he stepped back out with the guide following him. The bus driver climbed aboard, gave a toot, and the bus took off up the street. As instructed, Rose, Sandy, and Jefferson managed to turn away to avoid the happy snappers. The guide was a man in his early 20s dressed in a dark green safari suit with an 'Australia Zoo Beerwah' cap on the back. His long, blonde, scraggly hair was tied in a ponytail, and he had matching dark green sandals. He approached their small group and introduced himself: 'Hiya, I'm Billy-Bob Kingsman, but call me BB; you've got to love B.B. King. He was like the king of the blues.

'This is Sandy and Rose from the University of Queensland and our driver Bruce. If it's OK, we'll come with you tomorrow on the next field trip to look around. I've checked, and there's another tourist bus load due at eleven, so we'll hook up with them.'

'OK, but like fix it up with Kerry in the office. This is like her mobile number. I'll see you tomorrow.'

'Sorry, Mr BB, can I ask how much it is?'

'Sure, Sandy. It's like a hundred for the five-hour hike. If one of our group like finds the elusive tiger, we'll like take another hundred as it means we have found what we have been searching for over the last fifty years ....'

Sandy interjected. 'Eighty years, BB, the last known sighting was 1936, that makes it over eighty-four years.' BB nodded and continued, 'Well, you like know a bit about it then.' Nic looked over to Sandy, hoping she would stop with the questions to BB. 'Like I said, eighty-four years. Kerry only takes a Credit Card, so we'll add a Finder's fee, which means that this area will explode with tourists, so we have to be ready for that.'

They watched as the guide walked away, and Nic addressed his group. 'Guys, please don't ask him anything about anything. He would've already known we knew the cost, so hopefully, nothing more comes from it. Remember, in this line of work, we must know the known, unknown, and unknowns. We have to stay somewhere in between the known and not known.'

'Is he always like this, Rose?'

'Yes, Bruce, and remember it's not a date; it's a job.'

Their group made their way to The Tarkine Hotel, checked in, and after delivering their luggage to the rooms, went over the road to check out the animal refuge pens. BB was standing in the middle of the largest pen, fending off a couple of wallabies, trying to access the packet of seeds he was holding. He nodded at their arrival, moved over to them, and collected another packet of seeds from a quad bike trailer. 'These little guys don't bother you much, but watch out for 'Big-Red'. He's around here somewhere. Someone thought it was a good idea to smuggle a large male kangaroo in the back of a truck one weekend and leave it here. When the police finally arrived from Burnie, the dumb guys panicked and let it go into the scrub. It turns up occasionally and scares the crap out of you. It mainly stays around the hiking trail, so we generally don't see it up here as it doesn't like getting close to people.'

Nic's group moved over to the other pens. A couple of wombats were hiding in burrows, and another contained a couple of Tasmanian devils. BB nodded towards the pens. 'Don't go into either of those pens, as they are vicious little critters.'

'Which ones, BB, the wombats or the devils?'

'Both, Rose. The devils will chew your legs off, and the wombats will gnaw at your toes, then drag you into their burrows, have a party, and finish you off.' They laughed at him, but suddenly the devils started fighting, and the women stepped back.

Nic noticed the reaction. 'They're just discussing whom they are going to eat for dinner. Generally, it's one of the tourists that had got too close and fell into the pen. Is that right, BB?'

BB nodded. 'Hey, I like to use that line too, Dr Brown. It always gets a laugh.'

They left him tending to the animals and returned to the Hotel to enjoy a few pints of the local beers.

There was a roaring fire going in the Tannin Restaurant. 'Bruce' looked at the beer and sipped it very lightly. 'I can't drink this, Dr Brown; it tastes like they brewed it from the Tamar River, and Bruce only drinks the stuff they brew from the Derwent River. I'm from Hobart, you know.'

Rose looked at him. 'As opposed to the West End beer they draw from the River Torrens in Adelaide, or the XXXX Beer from the Brisbane River? Beer is beer and is free here, so cheers.'

'My sentiments exactly, Rose,' Nic affirmed, then added: 'but hey, I'm paying for it.'

Bruce again took over the conversation: 'I know the story of 'Big-Red', the kangaroo. There were a couple of guys that ran a boxing troupe in Burnie. They would bring it out to fight anyone prepared to join it in the ring. It got too big, so they just shipped it down here and let it go. The Police were too slow to catch them, making them hopping mad.'

Rose shook her head in dismay. 'OK, Bruce, I'll give you that one.'

At about 9 p.m., Rose and Sandy decided they'd had enough of the golf/war stories and realised Nic's only golfing claim to fame was that he had shot a sub-35 round of golf on nine holes of the Torrey Pines course on the Microsoft computer game. Bruce had finally had enough too. 'Nic, golf scores on computers don't count.'

In the meantime, BB moved inside the hotel onto a small stage near the bar and started playing blues songs on a well-worn acoustic guitar. Rose nodded towards the small stage. 'So Nic, will you get up and play like you did in Brisbane?'

'Probably, as it's just another way to check him out and gain his trust. You can always trust a musician.'

Bruce leaned in. 'Hey Rose, so Nic plays the guitar and all the other things, too? Are you sure he's not just Batman on holidays? Does he have a butler called Alfred?' Rose smiled as they watched Nic move towards BB. 'Nope, but we haven't even seen where he lives yet. I don't think it's in a stately manor with his surname on the front. Mind you, there is a suburb in Brisbane called Thorneside. Maybe Nic Thorn owns the whole village.'

The two men had a short conversation, and BB nodded to a second guitar case behind the stage. Nic opened it and extracted a battered old Gibson electric guitar. It was missing a couple of strings, but the case held some spares, so he re-strung it and plugged a cord into a Peavey Guitar Amp. They started with the song, 'That's Alright,' the Elvis Presley classic.

Everyone enjoyed the show, and the song stopped after about ten minutes of multiple alternate leads. Each had taken turns gyrating and lip curling for the small crowd. The audience called out for more, so they discussed their options. This time, it was 'When Love Comes to Town,' the song that B.B. King performed with the Irish band U2. BB was in his element, and Nic was struggling to keep up. Cheers and free beers were everywhere.

CHAPTER 7

Rose and Sandy were surprised at how well Nic and Bruce looked at breakfast, as before they had left last night, it had become deafening and a bit messy. They knew both men had moved on from beers to Sullivan's Cove, the local whiskey.

Rose swirled her glass of orange juice and took a sip. 'How do you do it, Nic? I mean 'the hair of the dog' and all that. When we left, you had an almost empty bottle of whiskey after more than a couple of pints. You must've been hammered.'

'Rose, what have I taught you about diversions and miss-directions? Before we started jamming, I noticed BB was in the restaurant, and he wasn't alone. Bruce and I ensured the beers stayed Cascade Light, and the near-empty Whiskey bottle on the table wasn't ours.'

Bruce nodded in confirmation. 'I liked drinking with this guy, Rose, and not just because he made me look seriously in the mirror; I'm also looking forward to getting to know him better.'

'That isn't ever going to happen, as our Nic is one very mysterious beast. Besides that, did you learn anything from BB and his cohorts?' Bruce continued. 'Well, I found out that the BB's folks live in Penguin, and he drives down from Burnie whenever the buses roll in. When he doesn't return, he sleeps in his Kombi-Van parked at the campsite. He's also committed to proving the existence of the elusive Tassie Tiger. Did I miss anything, Dr Brown?'

'Nope, apart from the fact that he doesn't seem to be making much money and he nursed his beer for nearly two hours. He's also sleeping in his car, so I don't think he is in it for the money.'

Sandy interrupted them. 'OK, is there anything for me to do today?'

'Yep, see if you can find more about BB. Don't push it; just be friendly. Hang around him and be interested. Also, see if you can find more about that old Volksy he is sleeping in. It looks like a classic, so that might lead to something.'

'And me, Nic?'

'Rose, you and I will wander around the campsite. Bruce can drop us down there, then he'll take a few hours off,' Bruce added. 'I'll return to Burnie and check out Billy-Bob's back story. You said you traced Kerry's mobile call back to a property up there, so it would be interesting to see what that is.'

'Yep, good idea. We won't need transport here as the tourist bus arrives around eleven this morning. We can return by bus if you're not back in time. Just remember to use the names and the back stories.'

Bruce then drove them down to the camp entrance, and they collected BB along the way as he was ambling along the road. 'Thanks, guys; sometimes, like I do this walk instead of bringing the quad bike and trailer. It's good to cadge a lift.'

'No worries, BB; Bruce will drop us down there and then take the Troopy to Burnie to collect some supplies. We were supposed to collect them on our way down. We want to join your walk today and check it all out. Can I ask you a couple of questions?'

'Sure, Dr Brown, like shoot.'

'I saw you talking with someone last night and overheard a couple of things. One that didn't make sense.'

'OK, I'm sorry. Was I like talking too loudly? I don't think I said anything bad, though.'

Nic laughed. 'No BB. One of the things was that you have only been doing the job for a couple of months. The other was that the man said they were expecting the tourist numbers to increase now as there had been a new sighting. My guys don't know anything about that.'

'No one was like supposed to hear that, but it's true. I managed to take the picture myself, but it like wasn't with a tour or anything. I just happened to be wandering through the track, checking the trail cameras, and looking at the other side of the Pieman River, and there it was. It was late afternoon, in the shadows, but the lack of sunlight affected the quality of the picture though. I was like about a hundred and fifty metres away, but something was there. I took the picture with my iPad.'

Nic nodded. 'You don't seem to be carrying it.'

'Nope. I don't like take it with me on the hikes. I just need water and my phone.'

'So where is it then? And how can you keep something like that a secret? I can't keep secrets myself at all. I am hopeless at all that stuff.' Nic heard Sandy chortle but didn't react, and BB continued: 'The guy in the restaurant, Griff, he's like my boss. He has it but keeps telling me I must focus on finding the Tiger again. I have to sell the experience instead of looking at something that might be nothing, but I swear, Dr Brown, it was a Tassie Tiger, and I like to think they are still out there. '

'OK, thanks, BB. Another thing is the trail cameras. How many do you have along the trail, and have they ever snapped anything? I assume they're movement sensitive?'

'Like there are about ten or so, and the latest version, too. Griff upgraded them before I came down to run the show. I'm not allowed to like touch them as he does all that. I looked at a couple of them just after I started, and somehow, he found out and threatened to sack me on the spot.'

The group had arrived at the entrance to the trek site, gathered their backpacks from the Troopy, and waved at Bruce as he left. They stood there waiting for the bus to arrive as it was due in about half an hour. Sandy interrupted the silence. 'Sorry, BB. I have one more question. Where does all the money go? I mean, three hundred a pop, and you get forty hikers, so that's around four thousand a visit?'

'I don't know. I don't take bookings. Kerry handles all that stuff, but I don't get much out of it. Have you seen where I sleep when I don't drive back to Burnie?'

'Yes, BB, it's a classic. What year? 'Seventy-Five?'

'Sandy.'

'Yes, Dr. Brown.'

'It's a 'Seventy Eight, and please don't ask about the money. That's what I want. It's the beetles.' Sandy realised what Nic meant with the 'money' statement referencing The Beatles song and that she may be blowing their cover, so she nodded a subtle apology.

BB continued: 'Yep, Dr Brown, it is a seventy-eight, and like one day I'll restore her to the beauty that she deserves to be.'

Nothing more was said as they heard the bus chugging down the road. They abruptly stopped in the campsite, and about thirty eager hikers filed out. 'This is what I don't like, Dr Brown. Too many people want a look, and I can't control the flow. Griff doesn't get it. It's like eco-vandalism at its worst.'

'That it is BB, and there are ways it can be regulated. Besides, you guys aren't the only tour operators down here; you seem to be the Johnny-Come-latelys. How do you get away with it?'

'You would have to ask Griff about that. I just run the walks and keep the punters forever hopeful that we find something. So, unless he like pulls out my picture pretty soon, I think it just doesn't smell right. His brother is the bus driver, and I think Kerry may be his sister too, but I haven't been game enough to ask yet.'

'OK, so you take the group for a hike along the track and up to the river, but that would only take about an hour. I think it's about a three-kilometre return trip. Where do you go the rest of the time?'

'Well, it depends on the group. I like either going anti or clockwise, and we stop to discuss the flora, the fauna, and a bit of Corinna's history. I talk about other sites around here, places to visit, etc. I like to talk about the local animals. Then, we stopped near where I saw the tiger and took a break. I hope and wait for another glimpse without blurting it out.'

Sandy was about to press the issue on his sighting again, but the bus crowd had now curled around them and were looking to start the wilderness walk. BB was in his element as people were throwing questions at him from everywhere, and he kept it all in order. He was very respectful and professional, just as Nic expected him to be. The bus driver had climbed back and in and was now leaving. Griff was nowhere to be seen.

Nic felt the presence of someone getting closer to BB and had seen the same man at the Tannin

Restaurant last night, so he was interested to know if he had also overheard anything. However, he directed his questions towards Nic instead: 'Well, Dr Brown, I've looked at your LinkedIn page, and you've been studying Sumatran Tigers abroad. What gives you the idea that studying large cats and our little marsupials here have anything in common?'

BB interjected before Nic could respond: 'It's like all about the animals that we share our world with, and yes, the last confirmed Thylacine was over eighty years ago. So maybe the little dude is still with us, and maybe he's not. We're making other fauna extinct, too, and you would like to know why one man has chosen to spend his life looking at cats and dogs. Then he comes here to look for a long-extinct beastie? I'm sorry, mate, get a grip.' The man looked a little embarrassed, and Nic smiled.

The bus passengers were herded into a tiered arrangement, and BB explained the safety protocols: 'Ladies and gentlemen, it's like spook city out here. Don't like to take the forest for granted, and don't venture off the path or lose sight of the two dudes in front of you. Please get to know them, as they may save your life. We will wander along the Whyte River Track, down to the river, and stop there for a break. Please don't go into the water; there might be platypi, and whilst those little guys like to nibble your toes, it's not good for them to eat human flesh. Watch out for snakes too, especially the Hoop-Snake.'

He paused for effect. 'So, are we all good?' Everyone nodded.

Nic leaned over to Sandy and Rose. 'I'll tell you about the Hoop-Snakes later, guys. They don't exist, but it's another great tourist story.' Nic also noticed the group was hanging on BB's every word as he continued:

'And so, dudes and dudettes, there is no guarantee that you will see the mythical, magical Thylacine or any other animals. If you want to see lots of animals, go to a zoo. This is like the outback, Tasmanian wilderness style. If you're not careful, it can kill you.'

Rose whispered, 'Wow, this guy is really good, isn't he?'

Sandy responded quietly. 'Yes, he is. In a young cub, rough around the edges, in a not quite Nic Thorn sort of way. He is endearing, though, isn't he? I mean a bit young but cut the hair, put on some shoes, and a nice suit, he might look OK in the morning after the night before.'

'Sandy.'

'Yes, Rose.'

'Eeww. You *are* acting, aren't you? Nic just told you to be interested in him and find out what he knows and doesn't know. Nic doesn't want you to start poking around that little bear. Be careful, Sandy, as the little bear might bite back.'

Nic softly smiled at the expression Rose had just used.

The expedition made the half-circle trek in about an hour, rested where BB had nominated, and any stragglers were kept in line by Nic and Rose bringing up the rear. Sandy was now up the front with BB, and a more challenging part of the hike started as the group needed to traverse a single plank and rope bridge over the Whyte River. Some of the hikers were reluctant to cross. However, BB assured them that the bridge was solid and secure. He even ran over it four times, bouncing high each time. The group made it over without incident.

Nic nodded to Sandy and Rose, saying that they should keep going. 'I'm staying over this side if that's OK, as my knee gives me a bit of grief. I'll be here when you return, and I have my phone. So, I'll be all right.'

'Your phone won't work out here, Dr Brown. There's no reception.'

'Thanks, BB, it's a Satellite phone, so it'll do the job if needed.' Nic watched as Rose helped the last hiker across, and as the group moved out of sight, he went back along the path to look at the trail cameras. Having previously noted where they were located, he wanted to know why Griff was adamant that they shouldn't be tampered with. Taking a picture of the first one in situ with his regular phone, Nic carefully clipped the thin black plastic ties holding it to the tree. The camera was much lighter than he expected, so nothing was inside when he opened the front.

There was no mechanism at all; it was just an empty box. He checked his phone camera for the position, re-attached it with new ties, and stood up, wondering what was happening. He checked his watch and guessed there were probably twenty minutes left before returning to the crossing, so he jogged down to the next trail camera.

A man was standing next to it. 'Dr Brown, I presume?'

'Yes, and you must be Griff, pleased to meet you finally. Billy-Bob Kingsman has told me about your little show down here, and it looks like you are doing everything you can to keep it all under control. Bravo. It is a wonderful opportunity to shine the light on your part of the wilderness. Well done, Sir.'

'Well played, Dr Brown, but please don't veer from the path back to the rope bridge. It is hazardous to be out here all alone. You never know what lurks in the undergrowth, and the little bear might bite back.'

Nic realised that this was the exact phrase Rose had used to Sandy when making the remarks about BB, which concerned him. Griff then turned around and headed back up the path the group had already come from. Nic took a deep breath, moved back to the rope bridge, and saw that about half of the hikers were already on his side. BB and Sandy were deeply conversing, and they guided the last group over the rope bridge. Sandy came up to Nic. 'Get what you needed?'

'Yep, but Sandy, please be careful. Something is happening here, and some people may suspect we aren't as we seem.'

Sandy nodded. 'You mean BB? He is a sweetie and loves his job and his outdoor office. He kept reminding the group about taking chances and life choices. Don't leave it too late, that sort of stuff. It was uplifting.'

'Just be careful and remember 'The Beatles' if it comes to that. Be ready to run, and it might not be you that's in trouble.'

Sandy nodded. 'Yeah, yeah, yeah, Nic. I remember 'The Beatles.'

The whole group made their way around and completed the circuit, and the tourist bus was waiting to collect them. Everyone was still enthusiastic about the experience regardless of the lack of animal sightings, and the obligatory tourist bus photo was taken at the campsite. Rose, Sandy, Nic, and BB then alighted at the Village, and the tourist bus headed back to Launceston. Bruce had now returned and again met them at the Hotel for pre-dinner drinks.

BB stood up. 'Good night then. It's a free day tomorrow as the bus isn't due again until next week, so Sandy and I are going for an early morning walk if anyone wants to join us. We'll take the Honda four-wheel drive buggy down to the river, and I'll show her some of the rock pools. The water is beautiful, clear, and great for an early morning bath. It's like bathing in cold tea.'

They all retired for the night, and Nic noticed Griff was still nowhere to be seen.

CHAPTER 8

The others had decided not to get up so early, so BB met Sandy at 6 a.m. outside the Hotel, and together, they rode the Honda ATV down the road to the Whyte River Track. They left the vehicle and started along the walking trail, taking it anti-clockwise this time, and eventually stopped at the rope bridge.

'Just up the bend, there's like the rock pools. The river is still there, and these little rock pools are along the shoreline. I've been here a couple of times. It's better when it's warmer, but it doesn't get above twenty degrees here anyway.' BB sloughed his clothes and plunged into one of the rock pools.

Meanwhile, Sandy had turned away and sat on the ground to experience the morning light. 'Come on in, Sandy. It's mighty fine. Like a cold cup of tea on a hot morning.' Sandy looked over. 'No thanks, BB. I'm good.'

BB splashed a little in the pool. 'Where's your sense of the wilderness?'

Sandy smiled. 'Swimming in cold water at six thirty in the morning isn't my cup of tea.' BB climbed out of the pool and stood on a large rock facing the river. He stepped down, gathered his clothes, moved towards Sandy, and stood together admiring the serenity. They were both looking across the river when suddenly, from the forest, the giant red kangaroo bounded towards them. They both froze as the colossal beast reared back against its tail and took an aggressive boxing stance. 'Don't move, Sandy, just keep still. I don't know how it's going to react. Watch out for its legs as he uses them to kick out. Get ready to run, just in case.'

Sandy looked over at him, unsure of their next move. 'I'd like to go back to breakfast now. I want beetles for breakfast, beetles, beetles, beetles.'

They started to turn around, and a black flash moved past them as someone or something sprung out from within the forest. Whoever it was caught the kangaroo with a rugby-style tackle, and both landed in the river with a big splash. Sandy went over and helped them out of the water, and in the meantime, the kangaroo was floundering in the river. 'Hiya Sandy. I heard Beatles and came running.'

'Thanks, Ni......Jefferson, it's you. You did this? How did you know the river was on the other side?'

'Actually, I didn't. I heard 'beetles' and thought you might need to be rescued. Being Jefferson means I may do things without thinking them through. It's a great feeling.'

BB had clambered down the slippery embankment

to rescue the floundering kangaroo and finally emerged with the exhausted animal. 'Hey guys, I'm like brown, muddy, stinky, and wet, and most of all, I've finally caught this big guy. Can you give me a hand, please? Hang on.... why did you call him Jefferson? I thought his name was 'Bruce'.'

Jefferson looked at him. 'Err, not here, BB, let's return to the Hotel. Nic will explain a few things. I'll help you carry the kangaroo to the quad bike. Will the trailer be strong enough to carry it back?' BB nodded. 'I've used it to carry four grumpy wombats and they weigh about the same as Big Red. Sandy, like grab the hessian bag and put it over the head as that should keep him calm for the ride.'

They manoeuvred the kangaroo into the trailer. Jefferson used the belt from his pants to bind the legs and tail together, and Sandy cradled the head while walking behind the ATV. 'Hey, BB, I've watched all the Skippy the Bush Kangaroo re-runs. I can speak kangaroo to keep it calm if needed. Tsk, tsk, Tsk.'

'Thanks, Sandy, but the kangaroo won't understand you. Skippy was an Eastern Grey from New South Wales, and this is a Big Red male kangaroo from Tasmania. It's a different dialect. Oh, and Skippy was a female too.'

Sandy nodded. 'Good point, thanks, BB.'

BB drove carefully back to the Hotel, and the trio trekked back to the village, untied the kangaroo, and off-loaded it into one of the pens. Nic and Rose came up to see what was going on. 'Jefferson just jumped into the river and took the kangaroo in. We've finally caught it.'

Nic hesitated, then nodded, realising their cover may be blown. 'Good job, guys.'

Sandy whispered. 'Thanks, but I blurt out 'Jefferson', which may have blown our cover.'

'I'll sort that out. Besides, Jefferson learned some interesting things in Burnie yesterday. Let's have breakfast and work out what to do from here.'

They all sat down together, including BB, and he had a couple of questions: 'So why is 'Bruce' also Jefferson? What's going on? Are you really Dr Brown, Sandy, and Rose?'

Nic leaned forward. 'Well, Billy-Bob, the short version is that we're here on behalf of the Tasmanian Parks and Wildlife Service. They are concerned about the increasing level of tourism in this pristine wilderness area. If left unchecked, it is eco-vandalism at its worst, as you said. So, when a group like yours suddenly enters the scene, bringing in up to eighty hikers a week, and there's a whisper of a new Thylacine sighting, people get worried. We are representing those worried people, BB; when did you get the idea that we weren't as we seemed?'

BB nodded. 'Well, it was Sandy, just a couple of things. I asked her about her biology degree, and she told me she'd studied at the Queensland University of Technology, but I knew they don't offer them there.

Besides that, no greenie would ever keep their finger-nails so well-manicured. I looked at Rose's, too, and they were the same. These two are just too stylish to be as close to nature as they like are supposed to be.'

Nic nodded. 'Good callout, BB.'

Sandy looked over. 'Sorry, Nic. I mixed up the known and unknown stuff.'

'That's OK, Sandy; not everything can be put into the brief.' Nic continued: 'Well, BB, 'Bruce' is Jefferson and Rose's brother, but this is all about maintaining anonymity. He went to Burnie and discovered a few things about Kerry and Griff you should know.'

BB nodded. 'So, is my job coming to an end then? Is it all a scam? I took that picture and truly hope the Thylacine isn't extinct. It's been like eighty years since we lost the last tiger, and we almost lost my little Tassie Devils with that nasty facial tumour thing.'

Nic put a hand on BB's shoulder. 'We'll need your help to get to your iPad and look at your photo. I know Griff is staying at the same place as we are. Where do you think he has it, and can I get to it?'

BB grimaced. 'Whoa, so you think this is all a scam then, as that would like be the end of me being a tour guide, too.'

'I don't know about that yet. Besides, I've heard from some of my guys that Griff is about to make a big announcement regarding a new sighting. He's also been buying up land on the other side of the Pieman River. It's all happening very quickly and too loudly for something that will devastate the wildlife as we know it around here.'

BB considered his options. 'OK, like, what do I need to do then? And whatever I do, I won't be working back here for a while, will I, Dr Brown?'

'Leave that one with me, BB; you can make a difference. Don't ever forget that whatever happens from now on. Let's hear what Jefferson discovered.'

Jefferson began: 'OK. You were almost right, BB. Kerry and Dallas, the bus drivers, are brother and sister, and Griff is their half-brother. The site that Kerry runs these tours from is a dog breeding farm. I didn't think that was odd until the neighbours told me they breed specific types of dogs, and many puppies are given up for adoption. They are trying for a whippet/corgi cross. The dogs are small, lean, and have a specific light brown colour. Some of them have been seen with black stripes along their flank. Are you getting the picture?'

Sandy shook her head. 'What's that, Jefferson?'

'Well, they're breeding a dog that looks like a Thylacine. Something that could resemble it from about one hundred and fifty metres or so and in the forest's shadows in fading light. It sounds like your photo opportunity, doesn't it, BB?' Rose piped up. 'So, all the stories about ducks are true, Nic. If it walks like a duck, talks like a duck, and squawks like a duck, it's probably a scam.'

'Exactly, Rose.' Nic leaned over and pressed his

forefinger onto her nose. Jefferson quickly interjected. 'Don't do that. She doesn't like it.'

Nic was about to respond, but BB interrupted the banter. 'OK, I get it, so let's get this guy. I'm in. He like keeps a large metal box under his bed, secured with those little TSA combination locks. I guess you can get into the room, but getting into the contents of the box is like something different altogether.'

Nic went all business again. 'Leave that to me, BB. The spare room keys are behind the Reservation Desk, so I'll need about twenty minutes to get in and out. Can you guys create a diversion?'

Rose groaned, and Sandy grinned. 'When?'

Nic smiled again. 'Right now. Let's give it thirty minutes to set things up. Griff is still around, but I heard he is checking out later this morning to return to Launceston to drum up business for the next bus load.'

BB sighed. 'Do you need my password for the iPad, too, Nic?'

'I would guess that it's 'Lucille'?'

Rose looked at him. 'How would you know that?'

'Lucille was the name of B.B. King's guitar.'

Rose nodded. 'So, what's the idea then?'

'Well, my kangaroo-capturing crusader, Jefferson, will get in the pen with Big Red, the boxing kangaroo, to see if he can go a round or two. Something about losing a bet at the pub last night, and then you two guys will get into a right old argument about the ethics of it. It has to be real, so you may have to throw punches. We'll have to get Griff out of the Hotel first. Rose and Sandy have done this sort of thing before with me.'

Rose shook her head. 'About four times, and every time you have been around somewhere to keep an eye on us.'

'Well, you're alone this time, but I'll have my deputy waiting, Jefferson. He'll make sure everything is kept under control, even if it does resemble controlled chaos.'

'OK, Nic. Another question if I may?'

'Sure, BB.' BB continued. 'I know he keeps a laptop in the box. How are you going to get into that?'

'Leave that to me too. I have people that get me the keys to get past any lock. In this case, I can access a USB with keystroke reading and password-breaking abilities. Don't tell anyone; they could be just a little illegal.'

Everything started to fall into place. BB found Griff still in his room and convinced him to come outside to discuss the boxing match between the kangaroo and 'Bruce'. Nic now had access to the spare room key. BB and Griff were now down at the animal refuge pens when 'Bruce' stormed up to them, remonstrating loudly: 'I need to speak with your little man there, Griff. He says I should not climb into the pen and take on the boxing kangaroo. I've got money riding on it.'

'So, I heard Bruce. Billy-Bob is filling me in at the moment.'

Jefferson began to climb into the pen, and BB stopped him, so he grabbed BB by his windbreaker, and they both toppled into the pen that held the wombats. The men stood and sized each other up; the kangaroo just looked at them and flicked its ears. Meantime, one of the wombats came out of his burrow, twitched its nose, and wondered what the commotion was all about.

BB tried to get up but was pushed down again, so he locked his legs through Jefferson's and brought him down. They started wrestling, and all the while, Griff was grinning. A second wombat came out and headed straight towards Jefferson's ankle, giving it a nip. 'Ow, that's not fair, BB. It's supposed to be man-to-man, not a wombat-wrestling tag team.'

The first wombat had now gathered courage and headed towards them. The two men were circling each other, all the while carefully watching their ankles. BB leaned down, grabbed the nearest wombat, and held it towards his opposition. 'Take your best shot, mate. I've got my little buddy here, and he's not happy that you want to take on his hopping mate over there. So, get out. Otherwise, I'll let him at you.' Meanwhile, the kangaroo had sat down, twitched its ears again, and enjoyed the drama unfolding. The men continued to circle each other, and the two wombats joined in, and then a growling noise started up from the other pen.

Sandy called out: 'See what you've started. Now, the devils are awake, too. Stop it, you two. Stop behaving like children. Especially in front of the children…oops…animals.'

A cry of 'enough' broke the scene, and Nic ran up. 'Get cleaned up, you two and meet me in the Restaurant in thirty minutes. Billy-Bob, get some clean clothes from your Kombi and use my room to get changed. Now move.'

They climbed out of the pen and slowly entered the Hotel. Nic moved over to Griff. 'I'm so sorry you had to see that, Griff. Would you mind meeting us in there, too, please?'

Thirty minutes later, coffee was served in the restaurant's private rooms, where Nic had a projector screen hooked into a laptop. Griff took a seat. 'So, Dr Brown, what's this show and tell all about?'

'Please take a seat and let me show and tell you.'

The first picture was the one BB had taken of the Thylacine. Griff nodded but said nothing. The second picture was of the dog kennels in Burnie. Nic then pressed the remote, and a picture of the corgi/whippet crossbreed scrolled through. The final picture was again of BB's Thylacine.

'So, what's this, Mr Thorn? I don't need to know how you got them, but so what? Yes, Billy-Bob has taken a recent picture of a Thylacine. I'm just waiting for my people to verify it, and I will soon release it to the public. It will be a godsend for tourism in this area. Big deal.'

BB looked over at him. 'It wouldn't be such a big deal if you weren't buying up the land on the other side of the Pieman River. I don't remember you mentioning that to me. Are you planning to like to build an Eco-Village over there, too? What happens to the wilderness around here then?'

'Not your problem, BB. Besides, you will go down in history as having taken the first picture of a creature long thought extinct.'

Nic then directed them back to the screen. This time, it was a close-up of the animal's side flank, only one side shot of the animal. Both the head and rump were across the screen. 'Well, Griff, look closely at BB's photo. I had his little photo scrutinised and found something interesting.'

'So what, Dr Brown?'

'Well, as you can see, Griff, there are fifteen or so stripes along the rump as expected, but between the stripes, there appear to be smaller, paler squares. Pale pink in colour. I have to hand it to you, Griff. This was about to be a perfect scam, but those little squares are your fingernails. I would assume that it's your hands holding the dog against your shins, then?'

BB stood up. 'You mongrel Griff.'

'Now, Billy-Bob, that is no way to talk to your boss, as you might need a reference from me; after all, you're looking for another job. And by the way, I think

I'll be going now. Please excuse me, and thanks for showing me your holiday snaps.' Griff stood up and strode out of the restaurant.

Jefferson stood. 'Do we need to go after him?'

'No, he doesn't have a car, and it's a long walk back to Burnie.'

Sandy softly sang to break the tension: 'In the jungle, the Tasmanian jungle, the lying scammer hides.'

The group then went over the details of the outcome of the scam, and BB was slowly shaking his head. 'So where to for me then, Nic? Thanks to you guys, there is one less scammer, but you have just done me out of a job.'

'Note quite BB, the Department of Primary Industries, Parks, Water and Environment has a vacancy for a full-time guide based at Burnie, so you might get the opportunity to travel a bit further afield than here. They are always looking for guides to run tours through Cradle Mountain, and your name came up. You start next Monday if you want the job.'

'Nice work, thanks, Nic.'

The group packed up the computer equipment, cancelled the rest of their stay at the Hotel, and then moved on to have an early lunch at the counter. They stepped outside, where BB took a deep breath and looked around. 'Hey Nic, my Kombi's gone.'

'Didn't you keep it locked?'

'Yes, but like the key was in one of those magnetic cases attached to the wheel rim. Griff must have seen me put it there. What do you reckon? He has like an hour and a half on us?'

'Yep, so that probably puts him almost in Burnie.'

'Damn, he like has my guitars too. I suppose I won't see them again either.'

Nic confirmed with the hotel staff that Griff had gone, so they all climbed into the Troopy and headed up to Burnie to track him down. They arrived under two hours later, and Jefferson drove them straight to the dog kennels. There was no sight of the Kombi, but evidence that someone had left quickly. Nic and Jefferson went over to the neighbours and came back.

'They are in the wind, guys. Old Mrs Kelly said Griff drove in, grabbed Kerry, threw everything they could into the Kombi, and drove off towards Devonport. The actual kennel owners are due back in a few days. They have been travelling around the mainland with their caravan.'

'So, we're off to Devonport? But that's not good.'

'Why?'

'Well, the Spirit of Tasmania ferry leaves from there back to the mainland, and you don't need I.D. to buy a ticket if you're a walk-on.'

'OK. I'll call Devonport Police and get them to visit the bus driver and the ferry terminal. Let's see what comes of that. I'll be back in a tick.'

They drove off towards Devonport, and Nic's phone rang halfway into the trip. 'Yes, thank you, Detective Rand, and sorry we couldn't get to you earlier.'

Nic turned back to the group. 'They have missed him too. He managed to get on an early flight back to Melbourne. Perhaps they'll pick him up over there. The Tasmanian Police are still looking for Griff and Kerry.'

In about 20 minutes, they arrived at the ferry terminal in East Devonport, then realised Griff and Kerry would not have been able to get on board as the ferry

departs daily at 9 a.m. Jefferson stopped the car. 'They must be around here somewhere. What do you want me to do? Just drive around and hope we get lucky. Look for a couple surrounded by little brown dogs with painted rumps?'

'Nope. It's all a Police matter now, and that's as far as we have to take it. We should head back to Hobart. It's about four hours away, so we'll return around eight. What would you like to do, BB?'

'I guess it's time to say goodbye, and I don't know if we'll ever meet again. Can you take me back to my folk's place? They live in the town of Penguin. It's a bit of a backtrack.'

They drove back to Penguin, where Rose and Sandy insisted on getting out of the car and going for a walk despite it raining. Nic called out to them. 'Where are you guys going?'

'We're looking for the penguins. The cute little dudes in their cute little dinner suits must be here somewhere. Otherwise, they could've just called the place 'Seagull.''

BB nodded. 'Indeed. The town was settled in 1861 and named Penguin by some botanist dude. The whole area was originally called Sulphur Creek for a while, but like that name stunk.'

The women returned after seeing the giant penguin sculpture on the foreshore and were wet from the intermittent showers. Rose looked at the men as she climbed into the Troopy and shucked her raincoat. 'You know, they should've named this place 'Raindear' instead.'

They dropped BB off at his parent's place, said their goodbyes, and headed to Hobart. Nic's phone rang again as they passed through Campbelltown. 'OK, thanks, Detective Rand, and good luck tracking them down. I'll call someone to collect it.' He disconnected. 'They've found BB's Kombi guys. It was dumped at the Abel Tasman Caravan Park in Devonport, but no trace of Griff or Kerry. I've arranged to collect it and will return it to BB.'

'Were his guitars in there?'

'No, nothing. It was stripped, just a shell by the seashore.'

Just before 8 p.m., they dropped Jefferson back home at Claremont, and both Eva and Emme came out to say their goodbyes. Rose presented Emme with a stuffed toy penguin. 'Thanks very much, Auntie Rose. I will call him 'Aye.''

'But 'A' is for apple, sweetie, not a penguin.'

'I wouldn't call him 'Pee', would I? That would be rude.'

Nic laughed. 'Wow, they start teaching the kids early with dad jokes down this way, don't they?'

'That's not supposed to be funny, Uncle Nic.' Emme hugged the new toy and twisted it side to side. 'Mummy and I are living back home with Daddy now, but please don't tell; it's a secret.'

'Hey, Emme.' The girl looked up at him. 'Yes, Daddy.'

'I am standing here, so it's not a secret if I know about it, right?'

'Oh.'

Nic, Sandy, and Rose then drove back to the Wrest Point Casino and, in the morning, gave a closing summary to the Department of Primary Industries, Parks, Water and Environment:

'Griff and Kerry had begun working on the scam in King Island and made a cash offer to lease the puppy farm so the owners could leave for the mainland. When they relocated to the site, that started everything in motion. Dallas, as it turned out, was an innocent bystander but guilty by association. They have since absconded and most likely are back on the big island north of here.'

As they left the car at the airport depot, Sandy looked at Nic. 'Game over? Another win for the good guys, Nic?'

'Almost, my Tassie Tiger twins, almost'.

CHAPTER 9

Nic, **Sandy and Rose** were waiting for their flights in the QANTAS Lounge at Hobart Airport. 'So, what's next for us? Is there anything exciting that you'll need the services of Miss Rose Palmer and Miss Sandy Fraser? Or how about Miss Adventure and Nancy Do-less?'

'Actually, nothing at the moment. However, we do have this meeting in Brisbane with the Collections Agency in a couple of weeks for Sandy. We can wind things up here and meet up later unless something else pops up from the Nic Thorn Scam and Fraud toaster.'

'So, just another flight of fun and frivolities with us back to Brisbane then?'

'Nope to that. I'm going back to Adelaide for a fortnight of cooking classes. I have a contact who runs an Adult Nutrition School in Hilton to help me brush up on my culinary skills for something big coming up in a couple of weeks. It's time for me to learn how to cook the books.'

Rose nodded. 'That's a novel idea, but we didn't

know you cook real food. We thought you were a takeaway guy through and through.'

'I can cook up a storm when needed to impress. Lamb fry is my specialty. There is so much for you to learn about me, my little gregarious green grass-hoppers.'

Sandy blurted out, 'Green? Why green? And lambs fry is the liver. That's disgusting.' Nic smiled. 'But aren't you green with envy? After all, I'm going back to Adelaide again without you.'

Sandy shook her head. 'Not exactly, no. We would be, though, if it were Hawaii or The Maldives, as you promised. What's for us to do now, then?'

Nic grinned. 'How about you head back to Bris Vegas, and tell you what, fly Business Class this time. My shout.'

'Thanks, but everything we do is your shout.'

'Well, there is that.'

There was a group hug, and they watched Nic board a plane bound for Adelaide.

Rose and Sandy returned to the QANTAS lounge to wait for their flight, and Rose pondered their current situation: 'Are we still OK with this thing we're doing with Nic? Did you ever think that we would be flying all around Australia, looking at all these places, and not having to spend a penny?

'Hey, that's not true. I just spent five dollars buying some nail polish. Do you want to see it?'

'No thanks, but be serious. When is all this going to end for us?'

'Don't worry so much. If everything falls into a heap, you could always go back to living with your parents; they might have someone else in mind for you to marry. Maybe not tall, dark, and handsome like Nic Thorn, though. Apparently, short, fat and shallow are your usual type anyway, at least that is what it says on your Vita Brevis Dating profile.'

'No, it doesn't.'

'Oh, yes, it does. Have a look.'

Sandy opened the link to the dating site, and there was a picture of Rose as 'Miss Panda-Eyes', a portrait photo posted from the GOMA site. The heading was: *'Tired of dating Goths? Please swipe right for Miss Panda-Eyes. You might be surprised. She likes her men short, fat, and shallow. NT".'*

'Damn you, Nic. He needs to know my password to make changes like that.' Sandy looked at her. 'Or maybe not. Remind me to change it when we return to Brisbane.'

Rose and Sandy had spare time at Hobart airport and found themselves in the Tasmania Beyond Souvenir shop. Sandy picked up a stuffed Tasmanian tiger toy and took it to the counter. 'Look, Rose, I'm using my credit card.'

The operator scanned the card, looked up at Sandy and took a pair of scissors from the console counter drawer. She cut the card in half and placed the severed pieces into the bin. 'I'm sorry, Sandra Fraser; the computer told me to destroy the card. You have to refer any inquiries to your Bank. Goodbye. Next, please.'

'Hey, hang on, that was my only card; it was an ATM card too. I can't get any money out now, either. What will I do about that?'

'Refer to your Bank. Next, please.'

Rose went to find her card. 'Here, let me get it. I'll put it on the business card anyway. Nic won't know; we can tell him it was for chocolate to calm our nerves. You still have the receipt for the nail polish.'

Rose placed the stuffed animal on the counter. 'How much is it?'

'Thirty-five dollars.'

'What? I don't want to buy all of them. You wouldn't have any left; then even your stuffed Tassie tigers would really be extinct.'

'Yes, it's thirty-five dollars for one, and don't give me any lip either. I still have my scissors handy. Snip, snip. Besides, some money goes towards tracking down the extinct Tassie tiger anyway. What a crock. Idiots say that something that died eighty years ago is still alive near Burnie.'

'It's closer to Corinna. We've just come from there and have been helping look for it.'

The operator looked past them. 'Idiots.... Oh, sorry, I don't mean you two. I mean, those people over there dressed as golfers. I hate that game.'

'Well, Miss Snippy-Pants, that's my brother and his

wife.' Rose finalised the sale and walked over to them. 'Hi, Jefferson, Eva and Emme. What's up?'

'We were hoping to catch you guys here. We have some great news, and it's not a little sister for Emme either.'

'OK, what's going on?'

'Well, Nic came through with his promise. The Club Wyndham Kona Resort was seeking a Professional golfer to run their Ladies Professional Golf Association Tournaments. Eva did the interview via Zoom when we were up doing our thing with the Tassie Tiger. They offered her the position, although she starts in two weeks, we have to leave almost immediately. I've already handed in my notice at Boags Brewery. Emme will have to change schools and is a bit upset about losing her friends, but we promised she would make some new ones.'

He took a breath. 'So, we need a huge favour. Would you guys mind staying in Hobart to get our house tidied up and the deal with the Land Agent so we can lease the place?'

'Sure, can do. Where's Kona? I haven't heard of it.'

'It's in Hawaii.'

Sandy laughed, and then Rose muttered. 'Damn you, Nic.'

The group returned to the QANTAS lounge, ordered a Dom Perignon, used the business credit card to celebrate their new life chapter, and raised their glasses to Nic when the bill came. Rose and Sandy watched as the two drove away in the Nissan 300Z. Eva was driving, and Jefferson was beaming.

Jefferson and his family flew out a day later, and Rose and Sandy were left behind to clear their place. They got straight into the cleaning and doing some minor maintenance. Sandy twisted her blonde hair into a ponytail and started wiping the countertop. 'Do you know if Nic paid Jefferson anything? Have we been paid for the Adelaide caper yet, either? So, who are we? The Nic Thorn volunteer workers?'

'I don't think that we need to worry much about that. Nic organised another card for us the other day, and they arrived in the post: two VISA debit cards as long as he keeps money in the account so we can access cash. Otherwise, we can use the business credit cards.'

Sandy shook her head. 'This is all starting to feel like we are two kept women; we don't have our own money or jobs. We don't have anything that isn't provided for us by Nic Thorn and Associates.'

Rose shook her head. 'But you still have your house in Brisbane, which you paid off with inheritance money from your Grandmother, and she left you some money on top of that, too.'

'Yes, there is that.'

'So don't worry so much. We could always go back to retail clothing and re-open 'The She Shed,' and as you've said if this Nic thing falls in a heap. I could go back to living with my parents, heaven forbid, but at least you have a home to go back to. Besides, have you checked your Vita Brevis dating site to see if Nic has made any changes to your profile?'

'Nope. Oh crap, what do you think he's done?'

Sandy quickly logged into the site, and the '*Sandra Dee'* song from the musical Grease started. Her caption read: '*Swipe right for Sandra D. She might not be the one for Danny Z. NT.'*

They were trying to work out how to log into the site to change the profile when the Real Estate Agent called and told them that if the house was cleaned up a little, it might get between three hundred and fifty and four hundred per week. Rose and Sandy arranged garden maintenance and cleaned the house inside and out. They also re-laminated the kitchen benches and painted all the cupboards.

Rose's phone rang just as they were staging the home - it was Nic: 'Hello, Angels. I'm just checking in. My business credit card bill has just been emailed to me, so I thought I would check that you have receipts for everything.'

'Hey, we know you don't do paperwork. Besides that, have you caught up with Driver? How is he driving you around, sleepy old Adelaide?'

'Nope, not this time. The cooking school is only about a thirty-minute walk from the city, so there is no need to go, and they have free bikes here. Have you finished at Jefferson's place yet? Any interest in the rental ads?'

'Yes, the Agent returned the other day and saw what we had done. She's saying we'll get closer to four hundred and fifty per week instead. Funny, what a bit of hard work does it?'

'Yep, so true. Have you heard from BB yet?'

Rose leaned forward. 'No, why?'

'He loves his new job and will be in Hobart tomorrow for a training session. He wanted to look you guys up, something about showing off his new wheels.'

'OK, send me his number, and we'll ring him. He can stay here too. We've converted the sunroom into a bedroom by sliding a wall around it. It's turned this place into something very practical.'

'No worries. Get BB to take pictures on his iPad and send them to me.'

'Very funny, you know that Griff took it. Did they ever catch up with him?'

'No, the communication between Tasmanian Police and Victorian Metro sometimes gets slightly lost. I sent him a new one and other things, like clipping shears to cut off his ponytail and some proper shoes. How can you not wear shoes in Tasmania? Your toes will drop off with the cold, and those Tassie Devils will devour them.'

'Tell us about it. We miss the warm Brisbane days but won't miss that appointment with the Debt Collection Agency. Anyway, the Agent has organised an inspection for this place later today, and the prospective tenants are golfers. They work at the Cadbury

Factory too, so we reckon we will be finally out of here by Wednesday.'

'OK, keep safe, and it's goodbye from me.'

They rang BB, and about forty minutes later, a horn beeped out the front. The duo stepped outside, and a gleaming, purple paisley-painted Volkswagen Kombi van was parked in the driveway. BB climbed out, gave a bow, and they clapped.

'Yep, like all thanks to Nic. Look what he did to my ride. It's not only pimped, but it is also precious too. A two-litre engine is rare, and some guy approached me at the Glenorchy BP Service Station to offer me twenty-five grand cash on the spot. I took his number and told him I would think about it. Also, come and check this out.' They went to the side of the Kombi van, and he brought out a guitar case, opened it, and showed them an Epiphone brand electric guitar. It was a B.B. King 'Lucille' model. 'You can't like get these here in Tasmania. I didn't even like to think they were in Australia. Nic bought it for me; I don't know why. Why did I deserve all of this?'

Rose smiled at him. 'Well, working with Nic Thorn and Associates, it's not what you do for us; it's what you do with yourself that counts.'

BB smiled and continued. 'Oh, thanks I guess. Sorry, I also like need somewhere to stay tonight, if that's OK?'

Rose nodded. 'All good, BB, just for the one night,

though. We're leaving tomorrow for Brisbane. We've finished here, and the tenants move in in a few days.'

They went inside, and BB updated them on the latest developments with Griff:

'I went back to the dog kennels in Burnie and told them what had happened whilst they were away, and if anything turns up for Kerry and Griff, they should inform the local Police. I also spoke to the Chief Ranger from the Mole Creek Animal Sanctuary and he would be happy for me to run their tours in my spare time. All of this because I helped you guys out. What a ride.'

CHAPTER 10

Two days later Rose and Sandy were back home in Brisbane playing with Dog, their eight-kilogram Maine Coon cat. Dave, the neighbour, had been looking after him while they were away, and Dog, being a cat, likes to eat whenever and wherever he wants. Nothing gets between Dog and his kitty dins, and he has no shame in going door to door looking for more affection and food. Sandy stopped patting the cat. 'What do we do until Nic gets in touch again?'

'I don't know. Maybe we should look into this house-styling stuff. Doing that for Jefferson and Eva was fun, and I miss dealing with people.'

'Nic is people. We've been dealing with other people that are his people, too.'

'Stop it, Sandy, as you're beginning to sound like him, and worst of all, I understood what you meant.'

After another week of being idle, they were again sitting on the rear deck sipping on Chardonnay and watching the sun go down. Sandy looked over the rim of her glass at Rose. 'C'mon, I know you want to. Let's call Nic to see what he's been up to.' Rose had dialled before Sandy could lift her phone off the table. It was answered quickly:

'Good afternoon. This is Tony's Taxidermy. You snuff 'em, we stuff em.'

'Nic?'

'Yes, Rose?'

'How did you know it was me?'

Sandy smiled. 'Your number would come up in his phone.'

'I can't get anything past you, Sandy, can I? What's up, guys?'

'Nothing. We're just checking in and ensuring you are returning for Sandy's bank thing next week.'

'Aw, you both miss me; that's nice. My awesome associates want to know how I've been.'

Rose shook her head. 'Something like that. So, what have you been up to at the cooking school? Have you been egg-spelled yet?'

'Well, no, but I have learned so much about eggs. Did you know that placing an egg in a water bowl and it floats to the top is no good? And if it does a little headstand dance on the bottom of the bowl, it should only be hard-boiled. How is that for egg-citing?'

Rose shook her head again. 'You're cracking us up. Seriously, what's this all about?'

'Well, there is a chance we'll be called into a food delivery scam, as something fishy is happening, like serving the wrong fish at a high-end French restaurant. A friend of mine has asked me to look into it with him. It hasn't quite come together yet. Do either of you speak French?'

Rose leaned forward. 'Oui. I spent a year in Paris as an exchange student in high school. I've also done a few terms at Alliance Francaise de Brisbane here in West End as one of the tutors. That was a couple of years ago, though.'

'Good to know, Rose.'

'What else have you been learning to cook then? French Fries, French Sticks, frog legs, Jambon au fromage? That's a ham and cheese sandwich, Mon Cheri.'

'Yes, I knew that, and it's not surprising that your car, the Nissan 'Scargo,' is so slow, as it's a snail in disguise.'

'That's an *escargot.*'

'Oui, listen, I'm catching up with Driver tomorrow, so I'll hug him for you'.

'You would do that for us? That's nice, but how will you find him? Is he still invisible like you told us he was during the Adelaide caper? We never saw him at all.'

'Nope, but he was impressed with you two guys, in any case. He said he enjoyed working with you and looks forward to the next time. That's another thing in the works, which involves log book discrepancies at a trucking company up at Port Augusta, so there might be a chance you will be coming back here to South Australia.'

'OK. We'll see you in Brisbane in a couple of days. So, it's goodnight from me."

They disconnected the call. Sandy brushed her hand through her blonde locks and took a breath. 'Rose, can you explain how Nic can do all this? How does he get paid to fly around Australia as he does? Can he bring his little posse along, too?'

Rose nodded. 'Nic is a free-lance consultant brought in to investigate all types of capers and scams, whether deliberate or miss-guided. He takes a commission from the larger capers, like the one in Adelaide, where the Insurance Company recovered more than two million dollars, or with the Pinnaroo recycling case, he charged a flat fee. He also brokered the sale of the Mercedes 300SL, which was worth more than one and a half million, so he made a bit on that, too. He told us when we met him that he buys, sells, does, knows, and loses stuff.'

Sandy nodded. 'So, it's all legitimate stuff then?'

'Yes, I guess so, but I've only known him for five hours more than you.'

'But you spent two days with him in Pinnaroo after the Adelaide Motor Show. Did you manage to learn a bit more about him then?'

'Not really. He was a true gentleman. We even stayed in different Hotels and streets. I had only the mosquitos for the company at night.'

'Let's make a pact; if either of us wants to take it

further with Nic, we both walk away and if *he* wants to take it further with either of us, we walk away too.'

Sandy nodded. 'Agreed. You've been my best friend for more than twenty years. I can't believe I let you go to Adelaide all those years ago. What a disaster that turned out to be, and I almost lost you forever, too. How do you want to do this? Spit on our hands and shake?' Rose smiled. 'No, maybe fill up the glasses again, and we toast to friendship. Although Jack Thomson, the Aussie actor, lived with two sisters for over fifteen years? What if it comes to that?'

'I'll think about it. I've thought about it, and 'Nup', but do you know that Jack was the first Australian Cleo women's magazine centrefold?'

'Eeww. He's like eighty or something?'

'Well, all his staples were in the right place back in nineteen seventy-two.'

CHAPTER 11

Rose and Sandy were getting worried as they hadn't heard from Nic since the call a week ago, and it was today that they were due to meet with the Collections Agency in Riparian Plaza. They gave up waiting to hear from him and were waiting in their Brisbane office for him to arrive. Nic arrived precisely at 3 p.m. as a stressed, dishevelled legal representative. He certainly played the part, even walking up to the receptionist, ignoring Rose and Sandy sitting there.

'Hello, I am Rickard O'Shea, and I have an appointment with Mr Paul Ryde. We are to talk about, um, Miss Sandra Fraser. Do you know if my client has arrived?'

'Certainly, sir, Miss Fraser and her friend Rose Palmer are sitting behind you. I take it that you haven't met your client yet?'

Rose stood up and made a faux introduction. 'Hello, Mr O'Shea, I'm Rose Palmer, and this is your client, Sandy Fraser.'

'Nice to meet you both,' then Nic looked towards the receptionist. 'I'm sorry, Miss um...sorry, I'm not good with names. Can we please have a room made available? I want to discuss this with my client before meeting with Mr Ryde. We'll only need ten minutes or so. I'm sure he wouldn't mind.' The receptionist stood up. 'Yes, that can be arranged. Please follow me.' They were led down a corridor and were left alone in an empty office. Rose and Sandy went up to Nic and gave him a peck on both cheeks simultaneously. Sandy put her hand on Nic's arm. 'We've missed you, and we're bored. Have you got anything for us to do yet? The French fish thing? Off to the Maldives?'

'Nope, nothing yet, but I've had my guys look into this Bank thing, and it all looks legitimate. When and where did you have your ID stolen, Sandy?'

'How did you know? Oh, that's right, you know stuff. About twelve months ago, I left it on a ferry one night after catching it across from the Jazz Club at Kangaroo Point. I had my hands full carrying stuff for my friend Carly; she's in the band with your drummer mate, Sticks Out. We got to talking about The Beatles being the best band ever. Did you know Paul McCartney was once asked what it was like working with the best drummer in the world? And Paul responded with Ringo wasn't even the best drummer in the band.'

'Yep, I've heard that one.'

Rose looked at them. 'I don't get it. Was the Paul guy the drummer or the singer? Wasn't he the one with the dark glasses and the high voice?'

'That was Roy Orbison, Rose.'

Rose smiled. 'Oh, I didn't know that Roy Orbison was in The Beatles.'

Sandy and Nic shook their heads in amazement, and then Sandy continued: 'OK, so what's my role here? Am I to pretend I'm someone else or something like that?' Rose nodded again. 'And I guess I play the muscle if it gets to that?'

Nic smiled at Rose's comment. 'Nope, play it just as it comes, but it could get uncomfortable. There's nothing Sandy has to worry about, she didn't borrow the money, so they can't touch her. He'll make you feel guilty and ultimately want the debt paid or whatever he can get out of it. I know you own your house and have some money in the bank. I'm thinking of taking my credit card back.'

Sandy shook her head 'That's not fair. I can't get access to my money at the moment. The woman in the Hobart Airport threw it away. I've been living on the bread line waiting on handouts from Dog.'

'True, but anyway, this is not one of our capers. This guy could be a handful, so remember when it doubts go to.....'

Rose looked at him. 'Tears? You want us to start crying in there?'

'Nope. I was never going to say that. When in doubt, go to Chocolate, and here, take these. Our time in this office is almost up.' Nic handed them a small pack of Haigh's chocolate-covered cashews.

Rose started to open the packet. 'Thanks, but when do we eat them?'

'My show, my rules. You can eat them whenever this guy pushes you so hard you want to start to say something. Instead of biting your tongue, bite the cashews, but don't worry, I have more packets here.' Nic opened the lid of his briefcase, and they peered inside. It was packed full of Haigh's chocolates and nothing else. There was a rap at the door; it opened, and a man held out his hand. 'Mr O'Shea and Miss Fraser, I am Paul Ryde. Follow me, and let's get this meeting started.' He had ignored Rose standing with them and hadn't even bothered to find out who was who. Rose was about to introduce herself, but Nic leaned to her and whispered. 'You can start the chocolates now, Rose.'

They were led to another office, where the man offered them a seat and took his own behind his desk. Nic realised there were only two seats and nodded for them to sit down. Nic then walked across the other side of the corridor, knocked on the door, noticed the office was empty and took the chair from behind the desk. As he shut the door and rolled it across the way, he saw it was from the office of:

'John Lannister, Managing Partner.'

The women shuffled up, so Nic pulled the chair beside them and handed over his Business Card. The man ignored the offer and began: 'Righto, Mr O'Shea, this is how we roll here. This debt is Sandra Fraser's, and unless directed to me by the courts, I will continue to pursue it from her. She can admit it here, and I am authorised to offer a debt arrangement. Otherwise, I'll continue to follow her for the whole enchilada.'

Rose was about to repeat something, so Nic subtly nodded to the chocolate cashews and noticed Sandy had almost eaten her whole bag. 'I'm sorry, Mr Ryde; please let me know when you're saying something worthy of my attention, and I'll turn my hearing aid on.' The man looked at him and was about to give a vitriolic rebuttal when Nic pulled a rolled portfolio of papers from his coat pocket and placed them on his desk. 'What's this, Mr O'Shea?'

Nic smiled. 'Read it and weep. I've always wanted to say that. This is a picture of the person who took out the loan in the name of Sandra Fraser at the Community Bank in Ipswich. It's also of them signing the loan agreement, which is a good security protocol, as the Bank takes a picture of the person borrowing the money. I wonder why they would do that. Funny too as my client, the real Sandra Fraser sitting here, is right-handed, whereas that person is signing with their left hand.'

The man stammered with his response: 'How did you get this? You can't access this information without the assistance of the Queensland Police or the Bank. You are neither with the Police nor is it a fraud. Which is it, Mr O'Shea?'

Nic stood up and motioned the other to do the

same. 'We're finished here, Mr Ryde, and thank you for your time. Please thank Mr Lannister for using his chair, too. I'll contact you in a few days to see how you want to continue this charade. The loan isn't my client's; she didn't borrow the money. I suggest you call the Fraud Team at Community Bank at 1300BANK. Have them also look at the other documents used to borrow these funds and where the bank statements are being sent. Goodbye, Mr Ryde, we'll see ourselves out.' Nic collected the two empty packets of cashews from the women, ushered them back out of the offices, and they exited the building.

Once outside, Nic took a deep breath. 'Thanks, guys, you played it exactly as we needed to.' Rose nodded. 'Doesn't all this secret squirrel stuff ever wear you out? And using the name 'Rick O'Shea'…. I almost burst out laughing.'

'I'm glad you noticed. I've used 'Ricochet' before, but that was the first time I got away without getting shot down in flames. Besides, all of this secret squirrel stuff is what I do in the search for the truth, justice, and the Milky Way.'

Sandy sighed. 'Is this bank stuff over then?'

Nic shook his head. 'Nope, not even close. We've only been able to get that picture today, and now the hard work begins finding and stopping them…and this time, it's personal.'

Sandy laughed. 'Oh wow, you just quoted from the

worst of the 'Jaws Movie, Jaws the Revenge, in '87. We watched it last night.'

Nic nodded in confirmation. 'Anyway, this is pure and simple identity theft, and unfortunately, it is widespread. Once the fraudsters get your ID, they can open a credit card or even steal from your accounts. Eighty per cent of people don't realise their ID is being used. We got lucky here, and they got careless.'

Sandy nodded. 'The thing that I don't get is how Banks, with all their security, allow things like this to happen?'

'There is always someone on the inside, and that is our way in.'

'So, this time, we're going after them. Whomever they are.'

'Yep, and we start with the guy who processed the loan application at the Community Bank at their Ipswich Branch. I've already made an appointment for eleven a.m. on Thursday. You're going to see if they will lend you money, both of you, to set up 'The She Shed' again, and during the interview, look around his office to see what things are there. Photos, service awards, that sort of thing. There's always something that doesn't look right or left as the case may be.'

It was Thursday, just before 11, and they were outside the Community Branch Ipswich. Nic's investigations had confirmed that the branch was the origin of Sandy's fraudulent loan. They had arrived in separate cars. Rose and Sandy were in their little Nissan Scargo. It was emblazoned with the decals of 'The She Shed.'

Nic had already been into the Bank to ensure the man interviewing them had processed Sandy's fictitious loan application.

Sandy and Rose were dressed in business attire, as they wanted to appear eager and professional and to be able to answer any questions about the business. A portfolio had been prepared with some factual information and some not. Nic told them he wouldn't be a part of the interview process at this stage.

The Bank clock chimed 11, and the loan arranger emerged from his little cocoon: 'Good morning, Miss Fraser and Miss Palmer; my name is Matt Seaford. Thank you for taking the time to meet with me today. Please take a seat. Would you like a coffee or anything before we start? And can I see some ID? Your driver's license will be fine.'

'No, we don't need drinks; thank you anyway.' They handed over the licenses.

'OK, firstly, I won't talk about the loan. Let's discuss your plans instead. So, you want to re-open your couture and coffee shop, 'The She Shed?' Just bear with me. I will do a business name search to see if the business is still registered, and we'll take it from there. Whilst that is happening, please tell me about yourselves. Are you together? Have you any children? Are you married?'

Sandy nodded. 'Rose, you go first.'

'I will, but firstly, Matt, can we talk about the loan process as we don't have much time today and didn't bring our information with us? We do have the Profit and Loss Statements from when the business was trading. Do you need any security for the loan? And we might need fit-out finance for the shelving, computers, etc.

The Banker held his hands up. 'Whoa, OK, you're jumping too far ahead, Miss Palmer. I need to ask you a question before we start. These licences show an address at West End. Why have you come down here to Ipswich? I mean, you could have gone into Brisbane.'

'Yes, that's true. A business acquaintance suggested we come here. We are considering if Ipswich is a viable place to set up the new business. Is that OK?'

'Oh sure, just checking. It's only a forty-minute drive down here from Brisbane, anyway. Good idea.' The Banker made a few notes, then continued, 'Now tell me about the business. Expected turnover? Have you made cash flow projections? That sort of thing. I will get your Personal Asset and Liability positions from you later. You need to sign a form for your Privacy Consent permission when we do our Credit Reference checks. Do either of you currently bank with us?'

'Nope, Sandy is with the Bank of Australia, and I'm with the Emergency Services Credit Union.'

The Banker nodded. 'OK, but you don't work with the Police, do you, Rose?'

'Nope.'

'OK, I will just key into our system just to check. OK, Rosemary Palmer, nothing under that, so that is good. Miss Sandra Fraser, OK, now that's interesting. We already have you on file; the same date of birth, but an address at.....' He looked at them, then at his phone on the desk.

'Can I see Matt? Do I have a doppelganger or something?'

'Err, no, and I am sorry, we'll have to leave it there. I've just received a text message that one of our Bank Branches has been robbed. I'll have to attend to it immediately. I'm the Union Rep, and we must ensure it's done properly. Please excuse me.'

The loan arranger quickly rose from his desk, moved out of the office, and shut the door behind him. Rose and Sandy sat there looking at each other. 'I can't believe he just did that. What do we do now? Did you see his phone ring or anything?'

'Nope, but Nic said to have a look around.'

Sandy nodded over to the Staff Award Nominations that were along the wall. 'Hey, this guy is an outstanding banker. He was the Community Banker of the Year and runner-up the year before. There's a chart on the side of the filing cabinet. It looks like they have a Weekly Home Loan sales target of half a million, and he is sitting around two and a half million.'

Rose's phone chirped. It was Nic and read: '?' So, she called him. 'What's up?'

'Well, your guy just scampered out of the building, made a phone call, jumped into a nearly new black BMW, and drove off. What did you say to him?'

'Nothing. When he called Sandy's name on the computer, he commented about her different address, looked down at his phone, promptly stood up, and left.'

'Is the computer screen still open?'

'Yes, but no, and we're not going to go over his side of the desk and play 'guess the man's password' either. That's your thing.'

'OK, just come out of the office. Ask someone else what happened to see what the reaction is.'

'OK.'

Rose and Sandy entered the banking chamber and met with the Branch Manager. 'I'm sorry to hear that one of your branches just got robbed. Do we assume our interview with Matt Seaford is also over?'

'He's left? And who told you we were just robbed? Is this a joke? We take our security very seriously here, ladies.'

'No, that's what Matt Seaford said to us. He said he had to go and left us in there by ourselves.'

'Mm, OK. I'm sure he will be in touch, and I apologise for the interruption.'

Rose and Sandy moved outside, went up to Nic's car, and he slid the window down. 'Back to my place at Southbank. Let's run over a few things.' Sandy tapped the roof of the car. 'Do we have to use the Bat-tunnel to get in there or anything like that? We haven't been there yet?'

'Nope, but you two are driving me batty with all the talk about me being Batman. I mean, maybe I could be Barry Allen as The Flash. I could save so much on petrol. Anyway, I'm at the Park Avenue complex, Apartment Sixty-Three. You can come in off the top of Grey Street. Call me when you arrive, and I'll buzz you into the basement car park.'

Rose nodded. 'What if we beat you there?'

'I have seen how you drive, Rose, and what you're driving, so I'm pretty sure I'll beat you there. If you're early, grab some wine from the local Hotel.'

Rose smiled. 'OK, see you then, and can you just wait until we start the car, just in case? The Scargo is getting a bit old, and we shouldn't be using it as a run-a-round. Do you have any ideas for two distressed damsels needing a saviour and a new car?'

Nic smiled. 'Hey, the last time you used that line was in Adelaide, and I had to buy the guy a Hummer because the guy got punched in the old schnozzle. You two aren't exactly Hummer sorts, but we can do car shopping when you get to my place, too.'

CHAPTER 12

They arrived at South Bank and stopped at the bottle shop purely for research to ensure their Business Credit cards were working correctly. Nic let them into the car park, and they parked next to his white Ford Mustang, then took the lift up to the apartment.

Rose was impressed with the view. 'How does a bat live with so much light, Nic? I mean, look at the view. From here, you can count the fruit bats living in the Botanic Gardens.'

'Yep, but don't open the balcony doors unless you want an earful of Captain Cook Bridge traffic, and it gets worse when it rains. It sounds like the whole world around me is sucking on a slushy.'

'Hey, Nic.'

'Yes, Rose.'

'Boo-hoo. What are you sitting on here, close to well over a million and a half in property value?'

'Something like that. My folks were one of the early ones to get in back in ' 'ninety-four, then I bought it off them about ten years ago, just before the last property boom. Let's not talk about money, honey. Tell me about the Bank stuff.'

Sandy interjected. 'Actually, I would like to talk about money for a second. How do you afford to keep all of this? I mean how do you get paid?'

'Well, Sandy, it's like this...ask Rose, and if you want a raise, buy a bread-maker.'

'Sandy.'

'Yes, Rose'.

'As I told you before, he buys, sells, finds, loses, and the next time we tell him to get stuffed, he might listen instead of shouting us a trip to Tasmania.'

Nic nodded. 'Where to begin? Well, your friend Matt Seaford's loan arranging has come to the at-tention of some significant people as too many loan numbers set off warning bells. So, whilst you were in the Bank, I was on the phone with Anya from the Australian Finance Authority. We've been given the green light to pursue the investigation.'

'Wow, Anna, as in the ex-State Premier and now the head of the Australian Finance Authority? You do deal with the top end of town.'

Nic shook his head. 'It's not the same, Anna. This is Anya—same show but never mind. We're catching up with her next week because of an AFA conference at the Brisbane Convention Centre at Southbank. I've been invited to give a short talk on Cyber Crime and ID fraud.'

'So, just in time to talk about this caper too?'

'Yep, and guess who else they have invited to speak?'

'The Batman?'

'Nope, but close, it's the Bankman - your new BFF Matt Seaford. After all, he's one of the Community Bank and Queensland's best home lenders. He will tell us all how you can still achieve Home Loan sales targets in this regulated and competitive market.'

'Yes, he steals people's IDs and probably signs the loan contracts.'

'Even more than that, apparently, his uptake of 'Spot and Refer' is one of the highest in the state. That's where he pays someone to refer them to a client and then pays over a 'spotter fee' when the settlement goes through. The Bank is happy, as they get a new client with a loan, and the spotter is happy as they get a kickback to whatever club they belong to.' Nic opened a folder lying on his desk. 'And in Matt's case, his uncle is high within the Brisbane Ice Hockey League, so money flows back there, too. He's had more spots than a teenager with a face full of pimples.'

Sandy nodded; 'That's both disgusting and interesting. I have a friend who plays Ice Hockey, and we call her 'Pucker' because she likes to kiss everyone she meets on the mouth. Not the fancy European double cheek thing you taught Jefferson; when you see her coming, you pray she didn't have garlic pizza for lunch.'

'Is there a point here somewhere, Sandy?'

'I'm getting to that. She said that someone from Community Bank had been sniffing around her team over at Boondall; they wanted to know if anyone needed a Home Loan and even left blank forms to fill out. I have one at home somewhere.' Nic nodded. 'Good to know and see if you can find it. In the meantime, open the wine, and let's go car shopping. My kind of afternoon. Let me know if I start driving you crazy with the car stuff.'

'Too late, we've already gone crazy for putting up with you for so long.'

Nic smiled and was setting up the laptop when his phone rang: 'Yes, this is Rickard O'Shea speaking. Thank you for calling Mr Lannister. I'm sorry to hear that Mr Ryde has taken a sudden leave of absence, but thank you for letting me know about the suspected fraud. Please keep in touch.' Nic disconnected.

Sandy looked at Nic. 'What's up, and how did you do that? You only have one phone and know to answer as Rickard O'Shea. How do you keep it all together?'

'It's not really that clever. I have all the numbers directed to this phone, and whenever the person rings, it comes up with the number they've rung, and the person's name comes up with it, too. If I don't take the call, they leave a message. Mr Lannister said he's contacted the Community Bank to sort things out and will be back in touch.'

'But the thing with all your names, like Rickard O'Shea? Is he a real person?'

'Well, the surname O'Shea is where it all started for me. Take a seat, and I'll give you a brief history from the book of the life and times of Nic Thorn, 'In the beginning...God created Heaven and Earth, took Sunday off, and created good and evil. That's where I come in.'

Rose shook her head. 'That's mostly from the bible.'

'Yep, a good read if you like books where you already know the ending, but I digress. Do you know the film 'Catch Me If You Can' with Leo Decap and Tom Hanks? It came out in '02, I think.'

Sandy nodded. 'We saw a re-run recently. Frank, someone became a lawyer, doctor, pilot, blah blah and defrauded the Banks with dodgy cheque stuff. Went to jail. You've based your life on a lie?'

'Nope, it was the FBI Agent, the real FBI Agent John Shea. He was the guy who got Abagnale out of jail and then set him up to help the FBI deal with the fraud. It felt weird when I met John as I was so starstruck, but here we are, and here we are, and here we go, solving scams as we hit the road.'

'I like it. I li, li, like it. That's from a song and a band that I do know.'

'OK, Rose. Hit me, baby, one more time.'

'Was it ABBA?'

'Nope, it was Status Quo, but I do, I do, I do think you were close enough. So, let's move on to cars before

Sandy falls asleep. Oops, too late, Sleeping Beauty is in da house.'

'What do we do now? Find a prince or a frog that can pucker up?'

'Nope, just tell me more about the bank thing before she wakes and wants to go home. Just how much wine has she had?'

'Um, I would say half a bottle. Anyhow, Matt Seaford was runner-up "Banker of the Year" last year, and this year, he's nearly two million over his target for weekly home loans. He carries two phones as a Union Rep. Well, the Branch Manager told us about the phones, but she doesn't know why he would need two phones.'

Nic nodded. 'OK, I think we need to use Sandy's 'Pucker' friend to get an introduction to see if we can get to him and maybe set something up using Sandy's place as security for the loan. We'll still work on the 'The She Shed' ploy but throw in a refinance of a Home Loan from a fictitious debt from another Bank. His eyes will bug out of his head.'

'How do we get around the Sandy ID thing, then? And that she doesn't have any debt?'

'I'll set that up too; just use her mother's maiden name. I've used something like that before. I'll also fake some bank loan statements. He'll probably be so eager to get it processed and approved that he won't even notice. How about I go in as Sandy's husband,

and you're my sister? You didn't give him any personal details yet, did you?'

'Nope, only my driver's licence; then he left before we got any further. So, is it back to Ipswich to scout for a new shop site?'

'No, it has to be somewhere else that he wouldn't necessarily check in detail, like Townsville or Hamilton Island; he won't care. We can ask for a Business Overdraft of one hundred and fifty thousand for the fit-out and forward charges on the stock. We could also talk him into giving us access to a lump sum upfront.'

Rose nodded. 'It looks like Sandy has settled in for the long haul now. She had a late-night gig with The Sweetened Plums and is probably catching up on her sleep. What is that couch made of? 100% fluffy duck down pillow?'

'Well, I like to lounge about when I watch my favourite sports like tiddly-winks and shuffleboard.' Rose ignored his comment. 'Anyway, tell me more about your hunger for this stuff. What was the first thing you can tell me that led you to the secret world of pros and cons?'

'You know what they say about it: make lemonade if the world gives you lemons. When I was a kid living high around Ouyen, I stayed with a friend in Mildura. His folks had a lemon tree, so we started juicing lemons, the old-fashioned plastic Tupperware way, and selling them for fifteen cents a glass. It was hard work cutting, squishing, and squeezing. You get the picture. Around the corner, another kid set up the same thing, but we didn't know where he got his lemons. He had them on the table, and they had the same juicer that we did, but he was popping the drinks out so much faster than we could and then undercutting us by ten cents. I got my mate's mum to go and look, and he was using lemon cordial. It was all a con. The lemons, the 'genuine lemonade' sign, everything.'

'So, what did you do, go over and beat him up?'

'Nope. We went there and asked him to stop selling it as real lemonade. It isn't good for our business. We told him it was a scam, that sort of thing.'

'And?'

'He said he would, then that night he climbed over my mate's back fence, cut the lemon tree down and took all the lemons.'

'That's a terrible story.'

'Yep, and ...wait for it... It's left a sour taste in my mouth ever since.'

'Hey, the next time I want to know anything about your past, remind me of this story, and I'll never ask again.'

'Duly noted. What do you want to have for dinner? It's already after seven; shall we wake the sleeping beauty?'

'Nope, just leave a note that we've gone to the Popollo Restaurant. She can meet us there. I don't expect she will go through your drawers or anything.'

They wrote the note, stuck it to her phone and went downstairs for dinner.

It was well after 9 p.m. when a refreshed Sandy arrived, and she slumped down at their table. 'What's up, guys? I feel I've been sleeping on a cloud. It was amazing.'

Rose nodded. 'So, can we call it a night? Let's escape this guy before he tortures us, threatening to return to his lounge and spend the night on it. If your couch is like that, what's your bed made of? Fluffy air?'

'No, it's water. I have a king-size waterbed, full motion, and everything. I know you both hate water and in the interest of keeping you dry, but you'll never see it.'

Rose stood up. 'Eeww, Nic and we're leaving. We'll see you at the AFA office on Park Road, Milton, in the morning.'

CHAPTER 13

The meeting with Anya at Milton was at 11 a.m., so Rose and Sandy caught the river ferry from West End. Nic was waiting out the front of the office, and they huddled together for a quick debrief. 'Now I know how disappointed you are that this is not the Anna from the AFA, but it is an Anya, so please don't make a show of it as she probably gets it all the time.'

'Yes, Nic.'

'And don't mention that you have set something in motion with Mr Matt Seaford either.'

'Yes, Nic.'

'And while you are at it, I would like you to join me at the Brisbane Convention Centre, too, but I don't want you to be seen with me. You will be there as walk-ins. It's a free show anyway.'

'Yes, Nic, and Nic'

'Yes, Rose.'

'We have decided on the new location of 'The She Shed.''

'Should I be worried?'

'Yes, Nic, but remember it was your suggestion. It'll be on Hamilton Island, in the Whitsundays.'

'Damn you, Rose, I was hoping you weren't listening.'

Rose smiled. 'Sandy and I listen to everything you say, especially after you barked at us for coming to your hotel room in Adelaide uninvited.'

'Hey, that was different. I have to keep my family safe. I know you aren't going to like this; I'm getting to the stage where I'd like to think you are my family, too.'

'Crikey Sandy, get me a bucket. I think I'm going to be sick.'

'Ah, Mr Creosote, from Monty Python's 'The Meaning of Life' Rose. That's one name I haven't used for a while.'

They moved into the offices of the AFA and met up with Anya. 'Thank you for meeting me today, Mr Thorn, Miss Fraser, and Miss, Oh my, I know you; I've seen the vision on the internet, it's 'Miss Panda-Eyes'. I thought he said you were part of his posse, but I didn't realise you would be here today, too. My young son has you on his screen saver. Don't you get sick of being told how funny that is, Miss Palmer?'

'I'm sorry, Anya, from the AFA, who isn't the real Anna? I don't.'

'You're right, you know, it's not that funny.'

'That's OK, Anya, it is actually. It's meant, as Nic's diversion at the Brisbane Gallery of Modern Art went off so well we are being inundated with more cases of fraud and scams to investigate.'

'Good point, Miss Palmer. So, let's get down to business. What do you have so far, Mr Thorn?'

'Thanks, Anya, but please call me Nic. Can we go to an office? I have prepared a portfolio for review, and we'll need your guys to be on board to ensure it runs as planned.' They were shown to an office and then made the presentation to Anya and her small team of investigators. 'You don't use PowerPoint? I could have set that up for you.'

'No, I don't, as anything on a computer leaves a trace. My guys use a storybook style to do these, and once the caper is finished, we shred it. It keeps everything much safer. Easily disposable.'

'How much have you been into this?'

'I've uncovered a few interesting things about Matt Seaford and the schemes he's involved in. He's accumulated two investment properties worth about a million, paid off his mother's home, and acquired a couple of cars worth around hundred and fifty thousand. All in less than three years, and for someone on roughly sixty-five thousand a year plus about fifteen thousand in bonuses, it's quite an achievement. He's not doing it alone, but I haven't worked out where his accomplices are. My two associates here, however, are willing and able to delve a little further, as required.'

Sandy leaned into Rose. 'I think he means us, Rose.'

'Yes, but I don't like delving into anything Nic

thinks we need to. It sounds a little bit scary.' Anya nodded. 'OK. We have five days to assemble this before your presentation at the Brisbane Convention Centre on Friday next week. Do you need us to do anything with that apart from our set-up?'

'Nope, it's all pretty simple. I'll run through the types of Bank fraud and how they can be mitigated. There'll be the selection of Bankers and people that agreed upon, too, and we'll have them talk about making the best of their opportunities. Then we'll chat with Mr Seaford to see what drops.'

'OK, but this is much deeper than we think. We reckon the Bank has brought in about three billion loans in the last few years. Someone in the Bank is disregarding what is going on.'

'Excuse me, Anya.'

'Yes, Sandy.'

'If you have only been looking at this Bank, how much of this is happening with the other Banks? Nic told me that most of them have an introduction Programme and are getting lots of business through Broker channels. How much of that could be fraudulent as well?'

'It depends on whether they are all complying with ethical business practices. All the Banks are well regulated, but we know from the findings of the Banking Royal Commission that some of their practices sometimes leave a lot to be desired. This might be a smaller player filling the void.'

The meeting finished about four hours later, and Nic's group went over the road to the Milton Coffee Club. They were all exhausted and were banking on a rest.

'It's now after three guys. Have you got anything else to do today?'

'Nope, but will you need us tomorrow as we're pitching an opportunity to a home-building firm, We'll be tendering for the business to be their stylists when they finish display homes and need them fitted out. We'll see how that goes, then talk to some Real Estate Agents.'

'Yep, that would be a good business model for you two. 'The She Shed' is rising from the ashes. You both have style and grace and would be good at it. Let me know if you want an equity partner. Have you done any business modelling as yet? I can help with that too; I have guys do that.'

'You said there that you're planning people only use drawings, not computer stuff?'

'So, you were listening? Yes, that's true for this job. I have many guys doing many things and others doing other things. That includes you guys doing your own thing.'

'Crikey, Rose. He's off with the gobble-dee-gook fairies again, isn't he?'

'He is, but the weird thing is I'm starting to under-stand him. Oh my, I'm beginning to get inside the mind of Mr Nic Thorn. Help me, please!'

Nic got up to move away, then leaned down to them. 'Guys, I'll call you to meet me where I'm setting up the rehearsal. It will be on Wednesday next week, so see you then. By the way, given that last nasty comment, you can get this tab this time.' Sandy smiled. 'Sure, we do pay our way occasionally.'

They watched him leave. 'Did you or Nic order anything, Sandy?'

'Nope.'

'Me either.'

CHAPTER 14

Rose and Sandy were home. It was early on Tuesday morning, and Nic hadn't yet rung. 'Are we going for a run this morning, Sandy? We'll need to start a fitness regime to be fully fit and alert for these capers that Nic keeps getting us involved in. Healthy body, healthy mind, that sort of thing.'

'Nope, but thanks for the offer. I went for a run this morning, down to Coles at West End for the morning muffins.'

'You took the car.'

'Yes, I ran down in the car, got milk, the muffins, and kitty dins for Dog.'

They were eating their breakfast muffins on the back deck, and Dog was munching his way on his crunchies when the cat suddenly stopped.

'Hey, somethings up; Dog has stopped eating.'

'Hello? Are you there, Rose?'

'That sounds like Michael, your ex and Dimond's husband. What do we do?'

'He hasn't met Dog yet, so he'll be our first line of defence.'

'Yes, Michael. We're here on the deck. What's going on? It's only nine in the morning.' Michael came towards the deck stairs and looked up.

In the meantime, Dog had moved over to the top of the stairs and was licking one of his paws. The big cat stopped licking and looked down at Michael. 'Can I come up?' Rose responded quickly. 'I think not, Michael. Besides, you must ask Dog if you can get past him. What do you want?'

'Well, firstly, to apologise for that day when Dimond was here. She was drunk and may have said something about us that you didn't need to hear.'

'Us, who 'us'? There is no 'us', Michael.'

'No, Dimond, me and the kids, us. There will never be you and me as an us Rose. Your new friend Nic Thorn reminded me of that at Albert's funeral.'

'Dimond didn't say anything that we didn't know already. What do you want?'

'Well, I heard you met up with a guy called Matt Seaford, and he's a friend of mine. Well, not really a friend, but I send him Home Loan referrals. Can you tell me why you went to Ipswich and his Bank?'

Dog continued to maintain his vigil on the top of the stairs, was now busy doing his ballet and licked his undercarriage with legs splayed outwards, occasionally pausing to stare at Michael.

'We went there as we're getting 'The She Shed' business re-started, not that it's any of your business.

Besides, do you remember Sandy's Ice Hockey friend, Pauline Tucker? She gave us the guy's details.'

'Oh yeah, 'Pucker', I dated her once. You know she kisses everyone in the mouth that she meets? It creeped me out. She kissed her ex-boyfriend hello, then returned to kiss me goodbye. I couldn't cope with that.'

'That's her, but there's nothing more than that. Besides, none of your business is whom we do business with. So please leave.'

Dog stopped washing and started to make his way down the stairs. Michael began to back away. 'That's a cat, right? You call it Dog, but it is a cat?'

'Yes, it is, and I wouldn't be standing there if I were you. His kitty-dins are stored below the stairs, and he hasn't had breakfast yet.'

Michael moved off quickly, keeping one eye on the cat, and then drove away.

Rose and Sandy went down the stairs, patted Dog, and thanked him; then Rose called Nic. 'Michael was just here. Where are you?'

'Bowen Hills is putting the BCEC thing together. What did Michael want?'

'It turns out he knows Matt Seaford, so he wanted to know what we knew. Matt uses him as a referral source for Home Loans. Michael works for an Accountancy firm, so it makes sense.'

'Now that you mention it, I saw Michaels' name on

Friday's invitation list for the AFA show. I wondered where the connection was.'

'Will that make it difficult for us to be there? I mean, he'll know us.'

'It'll change things a little, but I want you both there to see what happens at these Industry functions. Can you come to my office today, at about two o'clock? Drive along Gregory Terrace to the Ekka Showgrounds at Bowen Hills, and I'll have a car space available. Oh, and have either of you worn a disguise before?

'I don't think so, 'Miss Panda-Eyes' doesn't count, does it?'

'Nope.'

An hour later, they were driving in the Nissan Scargo slowly down Gregory Terrace and on the look-out for Nic when an older woman started crossing the street in front of them, pushing a Zimmer frame out in front of her.

They came to an abrupt halt, and then the woman raised her walking stick and thrust it towards them. Rose wove around her, stopped the car, and slid down the window to apologise. The old woman kept waving her stick, then moved to the back of the car, bumped into it, and called out: 'I've been hit, oh lord, I've just been hit.' The woman threw the walking frame before her and fell to the ground.

Rose and Sandy jumped out of the car to offer assistance, but whilst they were trying to help the woman, a young man ran over from the footpath, climbed in their little Nissan, turned the engine on, backed up, drove around their little group, and took off up the road. They didn't know where to look.

The woman stood up, took possession of the walking frame, and started shuffling towards the footpath, then gathered her skirt and sprinted away. They watched her go. 'What just happened? We lost the car.'

'I don't know. My purse and phone are in my pocket, so they didn't get that. What about you?'

'Well, that's my handbag on the ground. He must've dropped it out the window, so do we call Nic or the Police?'

They moved to the footpath and made the call; however, the funny thing was that they could hear a phone ringing somewhere close. Nic answered. 'Yep,' and the woman was returning towards them. She was on a call, holding the phone close to her face and covering the mouthpiece.

'Hey Nic, we just lost the car. An old woman and some young dude carjacked us and stole the Nissan Scargo.'

'Yep, I know. I saw it.'

'How do you know? Why didn't you stop it?'

The woman had come closer to them and was still on the phone. Rose saw this, so they nodded to Sandy, 'I bet that's Nic.'

'Twenty dollars, and you're on.'

Sandy and Rose deliberately turned away, intently

listening to Nic, then spun back and rushed at the woman, wrestling her to the ground, and the phone dropped from her hand. 'We've got you, Nic. Now get up.'

The old woman stood up; then Rose heard a voice from her phone. 'What's going on, Rose? Whom did you get?'

The old woman looked at them and smiled. 'Hello, I'm Sister Gwen. Nic has told me so much about you two, and he was correct; you are a couple of stunners. We just got you good.' She then cackled like an old witch. 'Tricky Nicky, you can come out now.'

The women watched as the young man they had just seen driving away in their car came out from the building they were next to. He was on the phone, so he disconnected. 'Hi guys, this is part of what happens out there. It's called the 'knock down, drive around' car theft scam. I hate that people do it, but it's certainly on the wane now, as the newer cars have tracking systems. Your little Nissan doesn't, so we thought we would try it to keep it in practice. Besides, you told me the other day that the car is not as re-liable as it should be, so I've decided to upgrade you. It's your bonus and all that.'

'Damn you, Nic.' This time, it came from Sandy, and Rose continued. 'Please don't take our little 'She Shed' car away, Nic. It's part of us and means so much.'

'Nope. I haven't done that; it's parked around the

back.' He whistled, and a new Peugeot 308 drove down the street, entirely wrapped in a vinyl wrap with 'The She Shed.' 'I heard your business was expanding, and you need a second car.'

'Nic'

'Yes, Sandy.'

'You once called me a wonder woman; I think you are a wonder man. Mm, that doesn't quite work, does it?'

Meanwhile, Sister Gwen approached them, still cackling like a witch. 'Hey, next time he takes you to Adelaide, don't jump in the Torrens. It makes you go crazy.' She then wandered up the street, turned into a corner and disappeared.

Nic looked at them. 'You two have made me realise that nothing is nothing if you don't do something for something.'

Sandy nodded. 'I agree with him, Rose. I am also beginning to understand Nic.'

'Thanks, Sandy. It's not that hard once you get to know me. Besides, it's been a while since I've let anyone get behind my façade. You two are the first outsiders in a long time. I like it, but once you get within the Nic Thorn nut-shell, you become exposed to the risks I take every time I do what I do.'

Rose leaned towards Nic. 'I think we know and like what we do when we're with you. It makes things seem more important. Bad people take down too many good people, so if we are the people who want to help you deal with all bad people, then it is for the sake of the good people. We are both for it.'

'Hey, Sandy.'

'Yes, Nic.'

'Rose is beginning to sound like me, too. I don't understand why, but I understood what she said.'

'Funny about that, but aren't we here for the Bank thing on Friday?'

'Yep, I've run through all that with my guys already. We'll have to work on your disguises now that we know Michael and Matt will be there. I think we can't have you being visible at all, and I don't have Harry Potters' Cloak of Invisibility or access to invisible paint, so we'll have to go to plan B. Who wants to be whom? The 'Grumpy Old Man' and 'Mrs Buxom Old Woman' disguises are available. You can go as a married couple if you want.'

'I'll go as the old man; I look better in pants anyway, and Rose can go as Mrs Buxom, as you have the bigger bust.' Rose looked at her. 'No, I don't.'

They followed Nic into the clothing warehouse in the building from where he had come after the theft. Then, they selected the clothing and latex masks and, after about an hour, presented themselves to the small group Nic had assembled for the banking show on Friday. Anya, from the AFA, was also there.

As Rose and Sandy re-entered the room, they both had hats on. One was a large flower hat, and the other was pulled over the ears. Both had their arms crossed and stood there with dour expressions, and their latex masks and age-spotted hands made them look the part.

Nic smiled. 'You look great, Sandy; the outfit suits you and works well. You might have to snort and say, 'What'd he say?' often. And Rose, Mrs Buxom thing suits you too. Weirdly, you look so matronly; you're far from it.'

Sandy responded as best she could through the latex lips. 'Thanks, Nic, but I'm Mrs Buxom, and Rose is Mr Grumpy Old Man. We changed our minds while in there as the double chin latex reacted with my face.'

'OK. So what else do you think we need to do for the show, Anya?'

Anya smiled. 'Oh, nothing. I just wanted to see how you put things together. It's my rostered day off, and you said you would be here today, so I thought I'd come over for a look.' Nic nodded. 'OK then, let's wind it up and see you all at eleven on Friday morning at the Exhibition Centre. My talk starts about two after our friend Matt Seaford does his thing. You two don't need to arrive until after twelve. We can't have a pair of old codgers falling asleep during the talks, snoring, and then dribbling on everybody, can we?'

CHAPTER 15

Sandy and Rose were already dressed and waiting at home late Friday morning. Nic had contacted them earlier to ensure they were still comfortable in the disguises. Sandy desperately pressed down on her tunic, trying to control it.

'Nic didn't give us any real names to use this time. Mrs Buxom and Mr Grumpy Old Man don't quite work. Woo-hoo. We can go as whomever we want. Any ideas?'

'I've always wanted to play Joh Bjelke-Petersen, the Queensland Premier from the eighties. Maybe you can go as his wife, Flo? Quickly, see if you can knock a dozen of her famous pumpkin scones by Crikey. You, you, you. Maybe we can chuck them at Nic for getting us to dress like this?'

'Nope, that won't work. You couldn't keep the 'ocker' Aussie voice up for that long; besides, what if someone recognises you as him?'

'You're right by jingo, by Crikey Flo. I'm dead, too.'

Rose grinned. 'Well, that definitely won't work. Let's go as a lovely old couple that has been married

forever and just like being with each other. They don't
need to say much, as they already know each other's
thoughts. Like the bald fellow, Professor X, in the Uncanny X-men movies.'

'Err, Patrick Stewart was Professor X, the mind
reader. The Uncanny X-men was an Aussie rock band
from the 'eighties, Rose.'

'Hey, I was born in ninety-one. Besides, I had a
mental vision of Hugh Jackman with his shirt off. He
does that a lot in those movies. It may have confused
me.'

'Yes, he did, and we had better eat something before we go. We might not be able to eat anything other
than mushed-up peas through these latex lips.'

Around 12:30 p.m., after scaring the bee-geezers
out of poor old Dog, they decided to take an Uber to
the event rather than drive themselves. They knew
the disguises worked as the taxi driver opened the
door for them and helped with the seat belts. He apologised to Sandy, who had to lean against her oversized
chest to secure the clip. 'What'd he say luv? What'd
he say?'

Sandy put her hand on Rose's arm. 'Shush. Don't
overplay it; he just wanted to know how old you are
and why you smell like moth balls.'

The driver dropped them off at the Brisbane Convention Centre in Grey Street, Southbank, so they
went into the foyer and found the rooms for the presentation:

'The Psycle of Selling.'

Fortunately, they saw Nic was waiting for them, but they couldn't attract his attention; however, Anya recognised them and played the perfect host by directing them into the auditorium. After guiding them to a seat, she sat down beside them. Anya then explained that there was currently a break between the presenters.

'Thank you, young lady; we aren't as quick as we used to be.'

'Are you Rose or Sandy?'

'No, young lady, I am Mrs Hawke, and this is my lovely husband, Mr Hawke. He doesn't say much as he's having a bad day and might have forgotten to put his teeth in. Besides, he didn't want to come out as 'Judge Judy' was on the telly.'

'Duly noted, and by the way, you guys look great for a pair of old codgers.'

'Mmmuth', Sandy offered, and Rose snorted.

Anya continued: 'Let me run through what happened so far. The show started at eleven, with each major bank's state 'Heads' giving their spiel about why their bank is better than the next one, both as a shareholder, lender, and depositor. That finished about twelve-thirty, so you haven't missed much; oops, I should not have said that, but you are both profoundly deaf anyway, aren't you?'

'Yes, young lady. What'd you say?'

'It's a longer break now for people to go and get

some lunch so that it won't start back up again until around one. Then the Banker 'wanna-be' CEO's prodigies get up and strut their stuff. I shouldn't have said that either; I'm so lucky you are both asleep. Anyway, the best of the best from each Bank will give a presentation for about twenty minutes. Like how they manage to keep up their momentum, our Mr Seaford will give his talk at two. Nic will come on after that.'

Sandy responded the best she could: 'It sounds like it's going to plan. Can you tell us if there has been anything new that you have learned? Is anyone doing anything different than the next Bank?'

'Not really; most of it has been about being flexible and ready to adapt to the client's needs and maintaining a social profile on Linked-In and Facebook. It sounds like Tik-Tok will be their next tactic; then they'll watch for the trends, that sort of thing. It makes you wonder why one Banker is more successful than the next. They all preach the same thing, 'it's not about price, it's all about service', but if they are all providing the same service, surely it only ever comes down to the loan's interest rate, which is the cost price.'

'Mmmuth,' came from Rose this time, and Sandy stood up to adjust her chest. 'I think that Mr Hawke has just seen Nic and is coming over here.'

'Wow, you guys are good. You understood that?'

'Yep, either that or Mr Hawke wants to go to the toilet. Hopefully, I'm right about Nic.'

Nic walked up, shook Anya's hand, then looked at Rose and stifled a laugh. 'You have the wig on backward.'

Rose poked out her tongue as best she could through the latex lips, and Nic continued: 'I managed to catch up with Michael just before; that's Rose's ex-husband from about ten years ago, Anya; she can tell you the story. He wanted to know what I saying about Cyber Crime and ID fraud. I haven't seen our Mr Seaford yet, but I suspect he'll just come in for his talk and then leave. A guy from another accounting firm is also interested in meeting with Mr. Seaford. He wants to offer up his clients as leads so his business can get the kickbacks. It makes you wonder where the client fits into all this.'

Anya interjected: 'Yes, that's the point, Nic. All the Accountants, Solicitors, Merchants, and Chiefs want their share of the lending pie. There must be a better way of supporting each other without compromising the benefit to the client?'

Nic leaned in. 'Hey Rose, here comes Michael. This is going to be interesting.'

Michael nodded as he approached. 'Afternoon again, Nic, and who is this pretty young lady with you? You are a lovely package, aren't you?'

Nic responded. 'This is Anya from the Australian Finance Authority, Michael.'

'And this lovely old couple? Are they your parents, Anya?' Nice to meet you all.'

Nic saw that Rose was about to raise the walking cane. 'No, Michael, we've just met Mr and Mrs Hawke. They've come here today to listen to Matt Seaford. They run an old folk home, and apparently, Matt Seaford could offer some incentives for Home Loan referrals to be paid back to the centre. Is that the sort of thing that you are doing from your accountancy firm?'

Michael gave him a stern look. 'Did Rose tell you that? If she were here, I'd have as few words to say. Yes, our business refers deals, but we trade in quality clients that need quality advice.' Michael then abruptly turned and left.

Rose gave him the finger, and Anya watched him walk away. 'That was your ex Rose? I'm so sorry, what a jerk.'

'Muufht.'

'My sentiments exactly, Rose.'

Nic responded. 'I think that means thanks, Anya. I can understand the old codger language. It's just another talent that I have.'

The crowd had come back in; there were around a hundred people in the audience, and in the meantime, Nic had pulled up a chair to sit between Rose and Sandy. Anya also stayed with their group. It was now nearing 1 p.m., and the emcee was ready for the next session at the podium:

'Good afternoon, Ladies and Gentlemen. I hope you enjoyed your lunch. The dollar was up, and the rates went down while you ate. Sorry, it's a finance joke. Anyway, our next speaker is from the Community Bank at Ipswich. He is the current highest performer for them, and at this stage, he is achieving a record high of home loan sales and referrals. Ladies and Gentlemen, Mr Matthew Seaford.'

There was a small amount of clapping, and Matt took his place at the lectern.

Nic leaned into Anya. 'Did you know that they had changed the order of speakers?'

'No, news to me. I wonder what's going on.'

Matt tapped at the microphone, removed it from the clasp, and sat on the end of the stage. It was apparent he wouldn't be reading from notes or using a PowerPoint presentation like some others had done. 'Hello, guests. I'm Matt Seaford from the Community Bank, and I have a serious confession to make - I'm a fraud.' The crowd gasped. Nic casually crossed his arms, and the three women leaned forward in their seats.

'Yes, I was told I was to speak about the psychology of selling Home Loans, but I can tell you there is none. It's a scam. There's no secret. There's no magic bullet. There's no reason why one Banker is more successful than the next. It is all about how quickly you can get them to sign on the bottom line.'

Anya leaned into Nic. 'This has suddenly got interesting, Nic.'

'Yep.'

Matt Seaford continued: 'Ladies and gentlemen. Can I see a show of hands, please? Who believes there isn't much difference between one bank and the next?' He waited, and about half the audience raised their hands. 'OK then. Who knows that there isn't much difference between one Bank and the next?' Less than half raised their hands this time, maybe out of confusion or to be seen to recognise that Matt had changed the one word.

'Semantics, it's all about semantics, Ladies and Gentlemen. It's not what you are selling but how you are selling it. For example, is there an older couple in the audience that would like to stand up for a minute? Don't worry, I'm not going to come down there, and you're not going to come up here either.'

Nic prompted Rose and Sandy to put their hands to stand up.

'OK, this couple, let's call them Mr and Mrs Retirees. They want higher interest rates to get a better return on their savings. They suffer when the rates go down and cheer when the rates go up, as they can buy that second coffee twice a week now. You can put your hands down now; thank you. OK, let's get another couple, this time a younger couple with a mortgage. Michael, are you out there? My friend Michael is here with his lovely young wife, Dimond. Where are you guys?'

Michael responded from within the room. 'Over here. I'm at the bar.'

Rose muttered. 'Crap, they are both here. She will surely recognise us.'

Nic responded discreetly. 'Just avoid her. I'll get you guys out of here early if I need to. Anya, you might need to create a distraction. Can you do that?'

'Sure. Does it mean that I might have to slap Michael?'

'I don't know, but you will have to get in line behind Mr and Mrs Hawke.'

Anya grinned at his response.

Matt continued. 'OK, thanks, Michael. This man here is one of my spot and referral partners. He gives me names, I give him money, and it's as simple as that. The more names he gives me, the more loans I can draw down, and the referral money flows back to his business. How's that for loyalty? We work together in our best interest, and everyone wins. The Home Lenders get a home loan, I get my sales target, and Michael's firm makes more money. What's wrong with that?' Anya whispered to no one in particular. 'Nothing until you start corrupting the process, Matt.'

Matt Seaford clasped his hands together. 'Well, Ladies and gentlemen, it comes down to this. Don't ever assume that your client, the one in front of you right now, knows anything about banking. It is your responsibility to tell them. Golden silences are key; don't speak until you are spoken to and they believe they win. It's all a chess game. A white pawn always goes first, but in the case of banking, always be the first one to sacrifice your pawn.'

Nic whispered: 'This guy is good, Anya. It's hard to believe that he believes in his success.'

'Yes, and I can't wait to bring him down.'

Matt was now strutting around the stage and had the audience in the palm of his hand. 'OK, guys, my time is almost up. I will leave it there, but before I go, can you queue the music, please, Mr Maestro?' Pink Floyd's song 'Money' started playing: 'Thank you, Ladies and Gentlemen. I have been Matt Seaford, and on behalf of the Community Bank at Ipswich, I hope you enjoy the rest of the event today. I'm always available to chat about your home lending needs. You know where I am, and you now know who I am. Let's do business very soon. You won't regret it.'

The audience started clapping, and some gave him a standing ovation.

'Nic.'

'Yes, Anya.'

'Can I slap Matt instead if you still need that diversion?'

The emcee shook Matt's hand as he stepped down from the stage and welcomed the next presenter: 'Thank you, Matt, that was very impressive, and I can see why you are one of the top performers across all the banks. I hope our next speaker, from the Queensland State Treasury, will be just as dynamic. Ladies and Gentlemen, please welcome Mr Bill Smithers to talk about Stamp Duty fraud.'

There was a soft groan across the group as the man set up the computer and his PowerPoint presentation.

CHAPTER 16

Nic kept watching Matt to see where he was going and whether or not he would stay. Matt went straight up to Michael, and they shared a quiet moment. Then Michael looked over to Nic, Anya and the two women, and the men laughed.

'Can I please go over and slap him now, Nic?'

'Which one, Anya?'

'Both of them.'

They listened to the new presenter drone on, and no one noticed when he finished and skulked away. The emcee then apologised that the next speaker from an accountancy firm had decided not to talk, so he introduced Nic instead: 'Ladies and Gentlemen, our next speaker is a consultant, and he will be representing the Australian Finance Authority. His topic today is Cyber Crime and ID fraud. Please welcome Mr Nic Thorn.'

Nic strode to the stage, started clapping, confidently ascended the stairs, moved over to the emcee, and began shaking his hand: 'Thank you, Adrian. It's nice that you've invited me to present on my topic of cybercrime and ID fraud, and by the way, your fly is undone.'

Adrian looked down, and Nic guided him to turn around simultaneously to provide some dignity, then turned back to the audience. Nic then showed him and the audience that he had a phone and wallet.

The emcee nodded. 'So Nic, you took my phone and wallet whilst I wasn't looking, very clever. Can I have them back, please?'

Nic grinned. 'Sure, Adrian, but if I gave these to you, it would be theft, and you could be arrested. They aren't yours; they're mine.' Adrian moved toward his suit jacket, checked for his wallet and phone, and true to Nic's word; he presented his cell phone and wallet to the audience. 'So, what's your point?'

'Well, part of my talk is about ID theft, and whilst I didn't steal your wallet or phone, I found out where you lived, your date of birth, and that you are about to change your home address.'

Adrian shrugged. 'Oh, so you came on stage earlier and had a look in my jacket?'

'Nope, you told me.'

'Oh yeah, we were talking before. You mentioned you were buying a house and wanted to know if I had had a good experience with a banker. I mentioned Matt Seaford. Then you asked me how long I have lived in Paddington, so I told you other stuff, too. I guess the rest was on Facebook or Linked In?'

Nic nodded. 'Yes, Adrian, a social presence is what

everything is all about. Loss of privacy is what you give up, though, Ladies and gentlemen, but just be aware that it is also the unlocking of all your secrets to the world wide web of wackiness. By the way, Adrian, next time you go on holiday, don't post the day your family leaves and returns. It makes for easy pickings for burglars, and as for working out your date of birth, on your birthday, your family presented you with a thirty-fifth cake. It was all on Facebook, nice family too.'

'Thanks for the lesson in social naivety, Mr Thorn, but everyone does it, and isn't that what life is all about? Sharing memories with everyone.'

'It is, but I would like to conduct a small experiment with the rest of the audience too, if I may, and this time, I will call for volunteers to come up on stage, but first again, I need a show of hands. Who amongst you has been the victim of fraud, or know someone that has been?' About half the audience put their hand up. 'OK, how about I re-phrase it? A few more of you mightn't think you have been defrauded.'

Nic pointed to the television screens:-

Credit Card statements have transactions that you don't recognise.

Mail you may be expecting (e.g. utility bills) never arrive.

Receipts arrive for things you haven't purchased.

Statements for loans or credit cards you haven't applied for.

You have been refused credit because of a poor credit history due to debts you have not incurred.

Debt Collection Agencies may contact you.

1-877-IDFRAUD (1-877-488-4888) or go to www.identityfraudtheft.gov/.

'Can I call for volunteers to come up on stage, please? Don't feel you have to. I want to personalise this a bit more. Can I please have three men and three women?'

Sandy looked at Rose, and they decided it wasn't a good idea if she wobbled her way up there, but at least fifteen people were making their way to the stage. 'I only have space for six, sorry. I know each of your stories is important, but I am also limited by time.'

Nic welcomed them on stage and was surprised as one of the guests making his way up there was Matt Seaford. Nic directed the small group to take a seat and started to work his way down the line. 'Please, can you briefly describe how you think the fraudsters managed to obtain your details? It's not a confessional, and if the perpetrator has been caught or is currently under police investigation, please simply say that is the case. Please don't mention names or exact dates.'

Nic went to the first guest:

'Hi, my name is Don. I went overseas and handed over my credit card to the hotel, and a month later, these charges started coming through. The Bank was excellent; all I had to do was cancel my card, and they refunded everything. It was still a hassle, and I was annoyed that my great trip was tainted with this experience.'

'Thanks, Don, next.'

'Hi, I am Linda. It's the same story as Don here. I paid for a family meal at a nice restaurant in Provence, France, and they took me for about five thousand. The bank got it all back, though.'

Nic looked to the audience: 'Thanks, Linda; however, the Bank didn't get anything back. They would have lost the money to the overseas merchant as the bank wouldn't pursue it in France. By the way, can I ask you a question about your credit card?'

'Sure.'

'Do you pay it off every month or just the minimum balance?'

'I try to pay it off, but sometimes make minimum payments. But why?'

'Well, the Banks are still charging over twenty per cent interest on credit cards whilst home loan rates are much lower, so they don't miss out. They are covering the cost of fraud by building it into the cost of the credit cards.'

'I suppose you are right, Mr Thorn'.

It was now Matt Seaford's turn. 'Mine is a little different. My father died around ten years ago, and he's buried in Brisbane at the Toowong Cemetery by the Milton Road roundabout. About four years ago, my mother received a loan statement from a bank showing he owed them fifteen thousand dollars. She was horrified, and it took its toll on her again. My Father was a proud man and didn't trust banks; he always dealt in cash. I checked it out and rang the bank. They'd allowed some slug to apply for an online loan using my father's date of birth and falsified ID. They never bothered to check any details. My dad had never borrowed money, so he had no credit history, and it took me years to sort it out. My mother still gets occasional calls from whoever has his file now, and I go through the whole process again. It showed me just how vulnerable the whole system is.'

'OK, duly noted, Matt, and thank you for your candidness.'

The next one on stage said the same story about credit card fraud.

The second to last one became highly animated once Nic presented her with the microphone as she burst into an impromptu version of the song 'Money, Money, Money' by ABBA, even doing the hair flicks. Nic struggled to take the microphone back from her.

She finally stopped and announced to the centre stage. 'Credit card theft is a victimless crime. I heard the sob stories from you chumps up here, and guess what? This is how I make my living. I steal handbags and purses and sell credit card numbers. So, thanks to the lovely court system, I keep getting let off with suspended sentences. You try and tell me that it needs to be taken seriously, you ignorant iguanas.'

The woman threw the microphone high into the air, leapt from the stage, landed in a classic super-hero crouched position, and then ran out. Nic tried to catch her but only managed to grab at her billowed coat.

The crowd watched as she ran for the exit; no one attempted to stop her, and the microphone landed on the stage with a loud crack. Nic picked it up, tapped it, and it was working: 'Well, Ladies and Gentlemen, there is that too. It's naïve to believe it is victimless. We build the cost of fraud and theft into everything we sell, and like our lady friend, there is always a back story, a reason that makes people do the things they do. ID Fraud and Cyber Crime can make a difference to your life in ways you never expected.'

Adrian, the emcee was the last one in the line. He stepped up and took the microphone from Nic. 'You too, Adrian?'

'Yes, Nic, mine started a long, long time ago in a galaxy far, far away. There was a little green man that resembled the ET dude in mini-me form.'

'Your point, Adrian? And it sounds like you watch too much Star Wars.'

'Well, I have to confess, the Star Wars merchandise got to me. I had to get the latest model, figurine, the latest.... You get the picture. So, just like our lady friend who just jumped off the stage, I used stolen cards to purchase them. It was an addiction, but the judge was lenient on me, so I'm currently making monthly restitution to a Collection Agency.'

Nic looked to the audience again. 'Well, this didn't exactly go how I thought it would, but Ladies and Gentlemen, I hope it has been short, sweet, and interesting. Mm, I have two close friends just like that. I have been Nic Thorn and wish there was more I could go through today, but time is our enemy. So, thank you again, and remember the best defence against cybercrime is you.' There was muted applause.

Nic left the stage, returned to the three women, and sat down with them. 'So how did I go? And what about the little reveal from Matt Seaford? Hasn't that thrown up something interesting? Or is it just his idea to show that he believes he is smarter than everyone else? But using stolen credit cards, as opposed to hundreds of thousands in fictitious home loans and referrals, are two entirely different things though, aren't they, Anya?'

Rose tapped Nic lightly on the arm. 'Aren't you going to go after her, dear?'

'Who?'

'The stage jumper. She confessed to all and sundry that she is a scammer and a thief.'

'It's already taken care of. My people are tracking her down.'

Rose sighed. 'People? What people? I thought Sandy and I were your people. Surely you don't expect us to shed our skins and chase her down. Besides, I don't have my Hush Puppy running shoes on.'

'Nope. I've sent a message to my runners, and they're off and running already, so to speak.'

Rose looked down at his shoes. 'I don't think so; you're wearing loafers. Aren't you at all concerned?'

Nic glanced at her. 'This is my concerned face, but you might be unable to tell as I'm wearing a latex mask.' Nic tweaked his nose, shrugged, then pulled his phone from his pocket and pressed on an app. It showed a street map of Brisbane and two flashing lights, one red and the other green.

Rose looked at it. 'You slipped a bug into her coat pocket.'

'Yep, green is for the good guys, and she is one in red.'

'What if she removes her coat?'

'Well, there is that, but did you see her coat? It's Armani, so she'll unlikely take that off.' Nic stood up and moved away from their group to avoid distracting the current presentation. 'I'll be back. Hold my seat.' Nic went outside and got his bearings on where the mystery woman was most likely headed.

In the meantime, the green and red lights were getting closer. The blip showed the woman was running southward through the Southbank restaurant precinct. Nic knew she would turn left to take the Goodwill pedestrian bridge that spanned the Brisbane River to access the Central Business District or keep running towards Stanley Street into the hospital precinct. Nic called the Police to see if they had any patrols in the area. However, was told they had limited resources to chase down an alleged thief, as there was a Climate Change march in the Botanic Gardens.

He was considering whether to take up the chase himself when his phone rang and as the caller was short of breath, he was likely the one giving chase. 'She's fast, but you were right to drop the bug into her coat pocket. I don't think she wants to take it off, and it must be slowing her down.'

'Head for the Goodwill bridge. I'll see if I can get someone on the other side, and we'll trap her in the middle.'

'Roger that.' The call was disconnected, and Nic made another call. 'Where are you? Can you get to the Goodwill Bridge?'

'Yep. What am I looking for?

'Somebody was running in an Armani coat.'

'This is Southbank; everybody runs in Armani, Lorna Jane, or Lululemon.'

'It's a full-length one.'

'OK, that'll make a difference.'

Nic looked down at the app. 'Yep, she's turned left and coming your way.'

'Roger that.'

The red and green lights were getting closer, and then they stopped. Nic's phone rang again. 'We've got her cornered. Well, she's stopped on the first lookout platform on the bridge. She isn't going anywhere. Do we apprehend her?'

Nic thought about the next move. He wasn't with the Police nor authorised to arrest or hold someone against their will. He also knew making a 'citizen's arrest' would not mean anything to this woman.

The caller yelled out from the phone. 'She jumped, Nic.'

'What?'

'Yep, she jumped off the bridge and is now in the water.'

'What about the Armani coat?'

'Well, she couldn't have loved it that much as she took it off and left it there.'

'Damn, we've lost her then. Did she survive?' The caller continued, 'Yep, and yep, but I feel for the guy on the jet-ski that rode up to her to see if she was OK. She pulled him off and is currently heading upriver.'

'Thanks anyway. We have no idea where she'll go from here. I'll see you back at the base later.' Nic returned to the centre and sat down, where Anya was the first to comment. 'So, what happened?'

'Missed her by that much. That's the bad news; the good news is that I have a lovely Armani coat if anyone is interested. I'd love to keep it, but it buttons up on the wrong side; however, it may be needed for evidence. What a shame, it's a beautiful coat.' Rose leaned forward. 'How did she get away?'

'She jumped from the Goodwill Bridge.'

'Oh, my God. Is she all right? I didn't think you liked to get people killed even if you're chasing them.'

Nic shrugged. 'I assume so, as she made a spectacular high dive into the river, then hijacked a jet ski and is heading upriver to who knows where. Anyway, we'll catch up with her later somewhere over the rainbow. Did I miss much?'

'Not really, the show just goes on and on. We've been discussing our next move from here with the bank thing. Haven't you just revealed yourself to Matt? I thought you wanted to be a part of 'The She Shed' proposal too?'

'Good point, but as long as I don't get to meet him as a client, you know, the old 'sorry can't meet with you', 'sorry out of town', 'too busy at work' ploy, it can be mostly done via email. Sandy hasn't mentioned my name yet, just that she was married.'

'Is that right, Mrs Hawke?'

'Mmmuth.' Sandy muttered whilst nodding at Nic.

'OK, thanks for letting me know that the latex is starting to get hot too, and you both want to get out of your outfits, but can you do one more thing for me?'

Sandy snorted, and Rose managed a muffled: 'Whenth huff we eva denied helping you Nicth?'

Nic stood up and looked over to where Matt was, and he was still standing with Michael. Dimond was there now, too. 'I'd like to see this Matt guy in action. Let's see what happens when I introduce Mr and Mrs Hawke to him and offer to broker a deal with referrals from old folks' homes. It might be best if you stay close too, Anya as you might pick up on something.'

Anya nodded. 'But surely, he wouldn't use them? The Banking Codes should prevent giving Home Loans to people who cannot service the loan. One hundred per cent reliance on rental income and all that?'

'Not really, but in a general sense, yes; however, there's always talk about Reverse Mortgages. Maybe there's a kickback to Matt if he sends those clients off to Solicitors specialising in that type of loan.'

Nic and Anya helped Rose and Sandy rise, and the four approached Matt and Michael. They were wary of Dimond being around, so Anya managed to move her away carefully. Nic led: 'Mr and Mrs Hawke, please let me introduce you to Matt Seaford. He's a Home Loan arranger at the Community Bank, and you might like to know that there is a Home Loan referral system. You refer someone to him who takes out a loan and he can offer a cash incentive in return, meaning he sends you some money back your way after settlement.'

Rose piped up. 'What-d-say?'

'Sorry, Matt. Mr Hawke is hard of hearing. I might have to run with this if it's OK?'

Rose/Mr Hawke nodded, and Sandy/Mrs Hawke grumbled, so Nic continued: 'OK, Mr Seaford, my clients operate a couple of Aged Care Homes and are interested in how the referral Home Loan scheme works and whether they qualify. How does it come together, and are there any repercussions for them if the loan defaults or anything like that?'

Matt Seaford nodded. 'No, nothing like that at all,

Mr Thorn. I sign them up as Referral Partners, and as long as they guarantee at least one referral a month, they'll qualify. Even if they can't, I can help them.' The comment piqued Nic's interest, so he pressed for more details. 'What's that supposed to mean, Mr Seaford?'

'Well, let's just say if their numbers are down, I can still send them something for just being a friend. I can access other Referral Partners that send me more than one a week. Everyone wins if one of theirs gets on-allocated to Mr and Mrs Hawke. Nothing is audited or checked as long the AFA don't know about it.'

Nic nodded. 'So, it is fraud then, Mr Seaford, isn't it?'

'Not exactly; it is just not kosher, but who cares? Neither is a lot of this stuff that goes on between banks. You can't convince me there isn't collusion be-tween banks regarding setting the interest rates? This isn't the place to talk about this stuff; too many walls have ears. Just leave me their details, and I'll be in touch.'

Nic wrote his number on a business card and nodded to Rose and Sandy, but Dimond and Anya interrupted their little group.

'Hello, Mr and Mrs Hawke. My name is Dimond, and I want to tell you about my parents. My husband, Michael, mentioned that you operate a couple of Aged Care Centres, and I'm looking to place my parents into specialised care.'

Nic looked at her, then at Rose and Sandy. 'I'm sorry, Dimond, not here, please; the old couple are getting tired and would rather call it a day and go home.'

Dimond nodded, then leaned into Nic. 'OK, but can you do me a favour? When you see Rose and Sandy next, tell them I want to catch up again for drinks on their back deck. I think I was a little sideways last time.'

Rose and Sandy started to move, then overheard a comment from Michael: 'Dimond, Rose and Sandy aren't here; that old couple were Anya's parents, besides, you told me you only like to hang out with beautiful people, and Rose and Sandy don't make it in my book.' Nic noticed Sandy and Rose casually raising their middle fingers as Michael and Dimond moved away.

The five returned to Nic's apartment so Rose and Sandy could remove their latex disguises and slough the 'old peoples' clothes. Nic started waving his hands in the elevator trying to get fresher air. 'Hey, Sandy'

'Yes, Nic?'

'A little less moth ball next time, please. It's a little overwhelming.'

'Sorry, but that's not moth balls; it's Rose's aftershave, 'Eau de toilet'. I'm surprised you didn't cop a whiff before. I guess you've been standing upwind.' They all sputtered and gasped, then quickly stepped out of the lift when it arrived on Nic's floor and let them into the apartment.

'You two can get changed in the spare room. Anya and I will run over the next challenge of dealing with Matt Seaford. Oh, and please don't go through the double doors at the end of the corridor. I keep a troll under the bed to keep out unwanted visitors.'

After about 20 minutes, Rose and Sandy showered and were presentable again. They collected the masks, clothes, and shoes and placed them into the boxes Nic brought from Bowen Hills. 'Let's have early dinner, but I think one of you might have to ring Dimond. I get a feeling that she was onto us even through your disguises. Make up some story about you having to get Dog his annual cat-flu shots or something like that. Just convince her that you were both somewhere else.'

'OK, I'll call her in the morning. Somewhere at Southbank for dinner again?'

'Yep, Anya is staying at the Mantra down on Grey Street and will meet us at the restaurant for dinner.'

Sandy nodded. 'It's so tiring being old, oops, sorry, you are nearly forty, aren't you, Nic?'

'Ha, ha. So, let's meet up again in the morning at my place around nine, and we'll go through a couple more things that Anya found out.'

Rose and Sandy took a taxi home, where Dog waited impatiently at the front door to be fed. Again.

CHAPTER 17

Rose and Sandy were back in the foyer of Nic's apartment complex, wondering how they could get up to his floor without his help. Fortunately, the maintenance man and his five-year-old son were about to get in the elevator, so they joined them.

'We don't have an access card to get to our friend's floor. Will you let us up there, though?'

'Nope, sorry, it's against policy.' The man swiped his pass, so they went back out, but suddenly his young son pressed all the buttons and smiled up at his father. All the floors had now been activated, and he looked to the women: 'Ok then, what floor?'

'Six.'

'All right, just don't tell anybody about it.'

They stepped to Level 6, knocked on Nic's door, and waited and waited. Finally, he came to the door, was shirtless, had a towel around his waist, and had damp hair. They didn't know where to look. 'Sorry guys, I was in the shower. How did you get up here?'

'We climbed the side of the building and swung in using our Spidey web strings.'

'I don't think so, Rose-Spiderman. The maintenance guy had his kid with him again, didn't he?'

Sandy was about to respond when a door closed
from within the apartment. 'My Spidey senses tell me
there's someone else here. What's that all about?'

'That's Anya. Just having a shower and getting
changed.'

A sound of 'Mmmuth' came from Rose. 'What's
that, Rose?'

Nic shook his head at them. 'Let's not do all that
again. Last time, it took you a year to get over that my
sister had been staying with me in my hotel room in
Adelaide.'

'We haven't known you for a year, Nic.'

'Yep, there is that. The truth is that Anya and I went
for an early morning paddle along the river as there
are canoes for hire by the grassy area in front of the
restaurants. Boy, do you guys know how to dampen
a guy's ego? I would have asked you too, but you are
both afraid of water. Besides, Anya is only twenty-
two and has a little tacker at home in Melbourne. Not
my scene.'

Sandy grinned. 'Well, we like to keep you safe. Besides, you said yesterday that a troll is hiding in your
bedroom. Hopefully, Anya didn't get attacked by it.'

'Nope, the troll is still in there, but sometimes he
gets lonely.'

Rose shook her head. 'Eeww, Nic, we haven't eaten
yet.'

Anya came through the corridor, was fully dressed, and smiled at them: 'Thanks for letting me use the shower. I enjoyed it, but next time I stay overnight, can I use....' Rose looked over to Sandy. 'He already told us, Anya. You guys went for an early morning paddle on the river, so there was not overnight, night stuff, with stuffing on the side.'

Anya nodded. 'Damn, you, Nic.'

'Hey, that's Rose's line, Anya,'

'I know he told me and also told me about you two and what you have been up to. The Brisbane Gallery caper, the Adelaide Car caper, the Tasmanian tiger thing, and Rose being held up by a broomstick gun. It sounds like you want to keep him on a short leash.'

Rose nodded. 'Nope, we're just happy to help out. After all, we used to sell cashmere capes when we had 'The She Shed' but still have a couple left in a box at home. Who knows, we might become the Caped Crusaders for the Common People. We could find one for you too, but they don't come in children's sizes.'

Nic interjected. 'Enough, you three. I am getting a headache from all of this.'

'Sorry, Nic, but Anya started it.'

'No, I didn't,' then poked her tongue out at them and smiled.

Nic continued. 'I'll make us breakfast; then we can get down to the business of the Matt Seaford thing. The pancake mix is in the fridge, and who wants omelettes?'

Rose wrung her hands together. 'Wow, Nic. A fully cooked breakfast, you must've learned something in Adelaide at the cooking school then?'

'Yep, the big secret is to have it all catered for, and you can't get blamed for tasting lousy. I had it delivered yesterday.'

They ate breakfast and cleared the plates. Anya and Nic each put a binder onto the table. Nic opened his first. The front page showed a list of Community Clubs across the greater Brisbane area. 'I've checked out the two-phone thing that the Branch Manager mentioned. Matt Seaford does have two phones. Chewy had to use up one of his favours with Optus, but all they needed to do was tell him two phone bills get emailed to Matt. One in his name, and the other in the name of…a Matt Steele.'

Rose grinned. 'Now that's a good made-up name. It sounds like one of yours, but what's the big deal there anyway?'

'Well, according to Anya's investigation, there was a Matthew Steele at the Community Bank in Ipswich. He left about four years ago and now lives in London.'

'And what's the connection to our Matt Seaford?'

Anya responded: 'Well, at the same branch, Matt Steele was Matt Seaford's predecessor. It looks like he just took his name. I assume that when someone leaves, the Banks don't destroy all the old business cards. So, Matt Steele has had his business stationery re-purposed by Matt Seaford.'

Rose nodded. 'So, that means Matt's accomplice is himself?'

'Nope, someone else must be involved; it's most likely in the Community Bank personnel area or some reporting line manager. Someone must have noticed something. I assume that as Matt Steele makes just as many referral claims, they must be archived somewhere.'

Rose piped up. 'Inside job, inside the inside job then. So how do we get to the inside, man? I've caught Nic Thorn gobble-de-gook speak, haven't I? It's scary.'

'Yep, but when you say something like that, it never sounds crazy. Unlike me.'

Rose leaned forward. 'So, what's with the list of Community Clubs?'

'It's a list of the Clubs with the Community Bank. Anya provided them, and I've been working through them. Nearly all of them have been contacted by Matt Seaford by phone, personal visit, or email. I've talked to a few; most are genuine referral sources. A couple of them had the documents he made them sign, which threw up something interesting. He made them sign two original forms, kept them both, and told them one was for his records. That gave him access to a second original every time. I assume he claimed it again somehow. Anya managed to get hold of copies of the scanned duplicates from the Bank's Audit Team. At the best guess, at least four hundred thousand in suspect claims over the last four years.'

Sandy shook her head. 'What a scam, and no one in the Bank has noticed a change to their bottom line either, then?'

Anya continued. 'Yes, and that appears to be the case. My dossier is different, however, as our Mr Seaford has lent money to someone and leveraged off their equity in the property. It works like this: Let's say your property is worth a million; the Banks lend up to eighty per cent against the first mortgage. So, if the first loan is for four hundred, he can get access to another four hundred. He, or Matt Steele, fraudulently processes the application, probably using the same application, the loan is drawn, and the loan statement goes elsewhere. I haven't worked out where yet, but it should be easy to track, as the Community Bank records will show where it will go. It is part of the Code of Banking Practice that a bank statement is issued at least every six months.'

Nic took over again: 'I also learned more about the referral process going through the Ice Hockey group. Matt's uncle has received about forty thousand dollars in referrals, and there hasn't been that much money flowing back to the club. Hey Sandy, you mentioned you know someone that plays Ice Hockey?'

'Yep, my friend Pauline, 'Pucker' Tucker. She's a little odd, however. You'll like her, Nic.'

Nic continued. 'So, let's set something up between your Ice Hockey friend and get Mr Seaford to run with

'The She Shed' proposal; then we can sort out who took that loan out in Sandy's name.'

Anya nodded. 'Actually, Nic, there's been a wrinkle in the Sandra Fraser thing too. You mentioned that Sandy doesn't have a mortgage, wow, at your age, that is impressive, but that's not the wrinkle, as it shows the Community Bank now holds a mortgage over her property.'

Sandy was shocked. 'What? How did he do that? That's ridiculous; he can't do that.... can he? I still have the yellow paper title at home. When it was transferred to my name, I paid it out, framed it and put it on the wall in my den.'

'Well, the Queensland Titles Office has gone paperless. Paper titles don't exist anymore. The one you have would have no legal value at all. There's a new property title exchange system in Australia, and that means it's open to fraud, too. It also means that someone may have seen the details on the title certificate in your den and used it to their advantage. I assume you have parties and don't know everyone in da house of Sandy?'

'No, well, I don't. I feel so stupid.'

Anya chipped in. 'Don't. It is what it is, but it might not be where it started from anyway. It could be from a Property Rates Notice you threw out, or the Title details can be obtained directly from the Queensland Titles Search site. All you need is the address and access to their online Lands Title system.'

Nic nodded. 'Anyway, what else did you find out, Anya? That's another wrinkle, but it sounds like it's not a Matt Seaford-caused thing. Someone else must be involved. They might still be using him and want to consolidate the existing fifteen thousand loan with a higher amount. If someone offers a property as security, it might give them up to eighty per cent of its value. The council valuation on Sandy's property is around six hundred, so we are looking upwards of four hundred and eighty thousand as a loan.'

Anya agreed. 'At this stage, the Community Bank won't tell me if there is any money owing, so you might be right there. So, depending on their policy on equity cash-outs, they might not even need a reason for the funds and hand it over.'

Nic concurred: 'OK, that means we might have to start getting things moving quicker. Did you get to download a copy of the executed mortgage?'

'Yes, I've got a downloaded copy. Here it is.'

They gathered around the document. The title search showed that the registered mortgage was lodged at the Title's Office on March eight, but it was dated January. The signature on the document was merely a squiggle.

Sandy was holding back her tears. 'Surely they check the signature against my driver's Licence or something?'

'But you lost that too so that it wouldn't matter. This is a fraud, so it's a matter for the Queensland

Fraud Squad. We will need to get Matt Seaford involved quickly. I think that we'll use the existing mortgage to our advantage. Let's give him a ring tomorrow and get back to the 'The She Shed' proposal. I will mock up a Loan statement with another Bank showing I owe around sixty thousand, leaving plenty of equity for us to access the one hundred and fifty to set up the business loan.'

Anya looked up from the folder. 'So, where is the new business being set up, Rose?'

'Hamilton Island, in the Whitsundays.'

'Whoa, good choice. I assume you have been there and checked out that you can open a couture/coffee shop on the island?'

'Not yet. Nic was sending Sandy and me there this weekend. We both need to recuperate from the shock about Sandy's mortgage. Don't we, Nic?'

'Sort of, but you've given me an idea. I'll get back in touch with the guys at my warehouse at Bowen Hills, and we'll set it up.' Sandy continued: 'So, we are going there this weekend? We haven't packed yet and will need to hold onto the business credit cards a little longer just in case we need the latest 'Agent Provocateur' swimwear.'

'Not exactly, Sandy. I'll get my guys to assemble a mock island/resort-style set at Bowen Hills in the warehouse, so you will appear to be there when you Zoom him in a couple of days.'

'Damn, you, Nic. He's promised to take us over-seas…eventually.'

Anya looked at both of them. 'Wow, I've heard he took you to Tasmania, and now you're off to Hamilton Island. He pays you to travel Business Class around Australia, you stay in the best Hotels, get driven around, and both still feel underwhelmed by it all?'

Sandy nodded. 'Yes, and that's why he likes work-ing with us. We keep him happy spending all his money.'

Nic shook his head. 'I know. If you were ten years older, Anya, you might've had a chance to join my little business, too.'

'Seriously, Nic?'

'Nope, sorry, Anya. It takes special types of people to get within the inner circle of Nic Thorn, and at the moment, there is only room for two others.'

Sandy nodded. 'That's great news, and just so you know, we don't take up much room, but we could always squeeze in someone else who is tall, dark, and handsome, too, if you needed to bring another him in. I've heard George Clooney is looking for another job now that he's finished filming all those 'Ocean' movie franchises.'

Nic smiled. 'Err, Sandy, let me think about that. It's now ten o'clock, so can you call Pauline and get something in motion? I'll shoot off my introduction email to Matt Seaford, and Anya needs to get back to her office at Milton to close things down.'

Rose looked over to Anya. 'We're sorry to see you go. Would you like us to drive you to the airport?'

'No, Rose, I need to tidy up only my office at the AFA Milton. I'm authorised to stay here for the duration of the investigation. It might take another two to three weeks, so paddle, paddle, paddle along the river with Nic every morning can continue too.'

Rose looked at her, then shook her head. 'Damn, you, Nic.'

Sandy called Pauline 'Pucker' Tucker and arranged to meet her at the Boondall Ice Centre at 2 p.m. They loved to have spectators as they had a trial game. Anya nodded that she could make it too.

Nic smiled, Rose noticed, and they watched as Anya left the apartment. 'Nic, are you smiling because Anya is now coming too? Or is it that you are going to meet the infamous kissing Ice Hockey player, known as 'Pucker'? Can I suggest you bring your minty mouth spray?'

'Nope, just you guys crack me up. The people you know and the things that you do when you are with or without me.'

'Thanks, Nic, we try, and that's why you pay us so well, too.'

'OK, well then, you guys shoot off home. I'll pick you up later, around one. Dress warmly.'

Just before 1 p.m., a car toot was heard outside their home at West End. It was Nic, in a black Chrysler 300C. They had previously been in the car when he picked them up at a West End restaurant a few months ago. He lowered the window and called out to them. 'We're off to the dodgy centre of Brisbane, at Boondall, so I thought I'd drive the ideal car.'

'That's not nice. If you keep that up, I will tell Pauline about you, and I don't know how she will react. She lives in Boondall. I'll say you enjoyed kissing her.'

The trip took about forty minutes, and Anya was waiting for them when they arrived. Rose and Sandy had black puffy jackets and woollen jeans for warmth. Nic wore a full-length dark navy leather jacket, and Anya wore a light jumper and jeans. She looked at the others. 'Hey, I'm up from Melbourne. It's going to be comfortable in there for me. I love the cold.'

The group stepped inside, and the cool air instantly hit them in the face. They acclimatised for a few minutes and were mesmerised by the Zamboni moving across the ice rink. Anya started to remove her jumper. 'Have you seen Pauline?'

'Yes, but don't call her Pauline. She might hit you or something worse.'

A roundish middle-aged woman started barreling towards their group. 'Here she comes, pucker up.' The woman made a beeline for Nic, grabbed him around the shoulders, gave him a big bear hug, and then planted a big smooch on his lips. He couldn't avoid it.

They stepped apart, and Pucker looked over to Rose, who was now trying to shuffle backward but ran into Anya. 'Come here, ya pretty little thing, and give me some sugar.'

'No, I'm fine, thanks.'

Pucker grabbed her as she did with Nic, who was trying to stifle his laugh and planted a big smooch on Rose's lips. 'Oh, you have brought someone else, Sandy. Who is this little plaything?'

'Hello Pauline, my name is Anya, and I am with....' Anya held out her hand. 'Sorry, did you call me Pauline?' She took hold of her hand, pulled her into a tighter embrace, and then gave a big sloppy kiss.

Sandy was next, and the others smiled, knowing what would happen. 'Hiya, Pucker, not today. I've got a cold, so I don't want to give it to you with your finals coming up and everything.'

'Hey, thanks, Sandy.' and she shook her hand. 'So, what's up?'

'Well, you said a guy recently hung around from the Community Bank. He was handing out forms, something to do with Home Loans and referrals back to the Ice Hockey Association?'

'Oh yeah, his Uncle Bill is high up in the Hockey Association too; neither of them is here today, but I have the key to his office. I was in there the other day, and there is a pile of those documents on his desk. I don't know who signs them. Our guys can't afford to buy hockey equipment. Is that what you came for? Don't you want to stay for the trial game too?'

'Sure, Pucker, it's hot out there today. In here is the best place to be.'

'Too right, follow me then.'

The group went through the arena, stopping temporarily to let the Zamboni pass after completing the scrape. It reversed, moved back onto the rink and started zipping around again.

Rose looked towards the team emblem on the back wall. 'Hey Rose, did you notice their mascot on the wall?'

'Yes, but what's it supposed to be?'

'It's a Maine Coon Cat, and it looks like Dog.'

Pucker overheard: 'Yep, that's the name of our Team. 'The Maine Coon Cats,' pretty clever, hey?'

The group was now at the office, and Pucker let them in. The documents were on the desk where she had mentioned, so Anya pulled out her phone and took some pictures, then Nic opened the folder and did a quick flick through. They were all signed, showed no names, and were otherwise blank. There were about fifty of them.

Rose also noticed the picture of the Maine Coon Cat behind the desk. 'That's our cat Pucker; we call it 'Dog'. Sandy and I couldn't agree on a dog or a cat when we went to the RSPCA and brought him home instead. Why does this Bill guy have a picture of our cat?'

'Really? Bill told me it was his, but I've been to his place, and there was no sign of him owning a cat. His brother died about ten years ago; maybe it was his. I know he still talks about it as if it was still alive. I just thought he had too many pucks in the head. He'd once said he had to give it away when his brother died. Do you have a picture of it?'

'Yep.' Rose opened her phone and pulled up the picture; they compared the two photos. It was the same cat; the only difference was that the image in the office showed the cat was on a leash.

Nic and Anya then collected about half of the incomplete referral documents and placed them into an evidence folder. Pucker was getting a little anxious from waiting.

'Got what you want, boys and girls? My lips are sealed. I won't say something to Bill or his nephew Matt. He runs when he sees me anyway, but I'll ensure I catch him next time. Pucker up, young fellow, when Pucker is in da house. So let's go and see Momma take down the game. 'Hoorah, hoorah.' Come on, you four. Give me a Hoorah, and Nic, you thump your chest a few times to motivate me.'

Their little group started chanting and followed her back to the ice rink. She disappeared into the change rooms about ten minutes later, emerged dressed as the goalie, in a full face mask, and fully kitted out in the Hockey uniform.

'She's the goalie, Sandy?' Sandy nodded. 'Yes, and that explains a few things. A few pucks go through the face grill, and she won't kiss anybody for a long time.

She would probably have to eat her dinner through a straw, too.'

Nic laughed. 'Yep. So, we have to stay and watch this. It could get bloody and toothy. I dated an Ice Hockey player once.'

Rose looked at him. 'Whoa, here's another insight into Nic Thorn's private world. Please tell us more, oh great sensei.'

Nic continued; 'Well, Xanthe was a Swedish goddess and also a champion figure skater. Her coach told her to choose either the team player or the skating. She had the potential for the Olympics, but the dream came crashing down when she broke both legs in her last hockey game. Her parents blamed me for being a distraction, and she blamed me for being so damn good-looking that she couldn't leave me alone. I took her to the hospital, and she never came out.'

Rose looked at him shocked. 'What? She died?'

'No, she became a doctor but dumped me before the end of her first day in there.'

Sandy smiled at the response. 'Poor Nic, all alone in this world, but at least you have the troll under your bed to keep you warm at night.'

They looked towards the game. One player had control of the puck, twisting and weaving, and headed straight towards Pucker in the goals. She blew him a kiss, hand movement only, and he took his shot. Pucker missed it, but it rebounded straight from the crossbar, shot back at him, and smacked him in the helmet. He went down. The small crowd cheered, then a fight broke out on the rink, and the game was abandoned. The First Aiders skated onto the rink towards the downed player. Pucker didn't get involved in the fight and skated up to Nic and his group. 'Cudnut hapenth toa betha blok'

'Obviously, no one liked him then.' Pucker nodded in confirmation.

Anya looked at him. 'You understood that, Nic?'

'Yep, she said, 'Couldn't have happened to a better bloke'. As well as understanding old people speak, I can do Ice Hockey mouthguard. It's just a gift, I guess.'

'So, what are we going to do then?'

'Well, back to your place this time. Let me look at the title document you have in your office, and maybe scroll through some of your party photos to see if we recognise anyone.'

'Are you coming with us too, Anya?'

'Nope, but thanks anyway. I have work to do at the Milton office, so I'll miss it. I'd love to meet your cat, though. Maybe next time.'

They all avoided taking a kiss from Pucker as they had suddenly all come down with the same cold that Sandy had, and although disappointed, Pucker agreed it was suddenly very contagious.

They were back at West End about an hour later, sipping Chardonnay on the back deck. Dog had, meantime, planted himself on Nic's lap. 'Hey, we should see if Dog takes to a leash. Wouldn't it be uncanny if your cat was the link to all this?'

'I don't have a leash, Nic, but I have a whip in my bedroom. Don't dare ask so that you won't be disappointed.' She went off and came back with a long leather stock whip. Nic was excited, and in his best Paul Hogan 'ocker speak' borrowed the classic quote from the Crocodile Dundee movie: *'Hey Sandy...'that's not a whip.....that's a whip...'*

Sandy tied a loop in the end and slipped it through Dog's collar. The animal didn't react, so Nic shifted so the cat would fall from his lap. Dog still didn't respond, and Sandy started going down the rear stairs, the cat followed and appeared to enjoy being on the leash. 'Yep, I'm convinced. It's the same cat.'

They walked around the neighbourhood, and Dave, from next door, joined in, but at the second corner, a little yapping Maltese terrier came rushing up to them. Dog stopped, looked at it, sat down, licked his paw, and Rose swore she saw the cat smiling. The tiny little dog then scampered away, yelping frantically. After the walk, Nic bade them farewell. 'We'll all meet again at Bowen Hills tomorrow.'

They watched Nic drive off, then realised that he hadn't looked at the Title Certificate or any photos, so Rose and Sandy decided to go through them. They started with the New Year's Eve party, as that was around the time when Sandy lost her ID. 'I've found something. I don't remember the guy at all, but almost

every photo of this guy has him near or holding Dog.
He does look familiar, though.'

'You bet he does. It's Mr Matt Seaford from the
Bank. No wonder he ran out of his office looking
worried.'

They sent a text to Nic, but he didn't respond.

CHAPTER 18

In the morning, Sandy went through their emails and saw that Nic had put together a domain name, 'The She Shed.com.au,' and a Twitter handle for them. 'Hey Rose, it looks like we've got a go-ahead from the Real Estate business. We won that tender that we did for one of their display properties at Brookwater Golf Estate. This could be the reincarnation that we are looking for.'

They high-fived.

'But there's a slight problem. We don't have access to any display furniture or know how or where to lease it. I bet Nic does, but he still didn't answer your text, did he?'

'Nup.'

'When are we supposed to be meeting him?'

'He just said tomorrow. Let's go now, then.'

They jumped into the new 'She Shed' Peugeot and went to Nic's warehouse/office at Bowen Hills. Anya was standing outside when they arrived.

'She keeps turning up, doesn't she?'

'Yes, but it's her show too. Soon, she will be back in Melbourne, and we'll have Nic all to ourselves again.'

'It's weird. This thing with Nic. Are you feeling the same stuff? You know, every time you see him, it makes your day? And you think about him when he is not here, and when he is …well.'

'So, what do we do about it?'

'Nothing, just keep holding on until it ends, and when it's over, we return to being us again. Can you put up with me for the duration?'

'Yes, so let's get this show on the road. I even bought a new swimming outfit for the opening of 'The She Shed' on Hamilton Island.'

'Hey, so did I.'

'Did you use Nic's Business Credit Card?'

'Yep.'

'Me too.'

'Are you going to wear it for the Zoom call?'

'Nope.'

'Me either.'

Rose and Sandy stepped out of the car and into the warehouse. It was set up as a resort-style retail outlet with fake palm trees and sand and people wandering around dressed in Tommy Bahama clothing.

Nic was directing the show, and Anya stood in the middle, sipping on a coffee. She looked over, waved at them, and moved forward. 'This is the new 'She Shed' on Hamilton Island, guys. The fit-out is almost complete. We have the latest La Marzocco Linear

Mini Coffee Maker, worth about seven grand. It's not plugged in or anything and won't be working. We can make it appear that it makes coffee but don't drink it. We will need you to stock some of the shelves from your stuff, or Nic might let you buy some outfits if you're nice to me.'

Nic finally came over and led the women into the mock shop. 'This'll work as long as we keep the Zoom call fairly short. He has to believe you are desperate for the money and must pay your fit-out and suppliers quickly. Put these earphones in here, and you can hear my direction leads.'

'When do we go live?'

'On Saturday. I don't think Matt will be in the Ipswich office. He might be playing a sport or catching a smooch from Pucker. Oh, and by the way, can you bring a picture of Dog too?'

'What for? Dog likes to be given a couple of days' notice before he does any modelling. It could turn into a catastrophe otherwise.'

'Hey, that's funny, Rose. We will subtly put it in the background of one of the Zoom links. It just might be the thing to bring down the house of Matt.'

'Sure thing. It is such a big ask of you, but we think we can find the time. We must assemble a display home fit-out, buy some clothes, and might even need a hand with the furniture and stuff.'

'Hey, Nic.'

'Yes, Anya.'

'Surely you're not going to fall for that as they don't have any leverage.'

Nic leaned into Anya and whispered. 'I know, and they don't know that it's my house at Brookwater that they are staging for. I'm selling it via one of my Property Trusts.' He leaned back and faced Rose and Sandy. 'Righto, you're on.'

'Hey Nic, you know that we heard that comment to Anya. You gave us the earphones, and we're still miked up.'

'Yep, I knew that. I'm putting a very rough script together that I'd like you to follow. As long as Matt knows how quickly you need access to the funds, he might arrange a business overdraft immediately.'

'OK. Did you get our text last night about what we found in the party photos?'

'Yep.'

'But you didn't reply.'

'Nope. I knew we were meeting this morning, and it's all coming full circle. The cat with Matt could all be the fat link to this, and his confession at the AFA presentation made it even more interesting. I would guess it's all got out of control for him, and the leash is starting to tighten around his neck.'

'So, who is the left-handed woman Matt signed the loan documents with?'

Anya sighed. 'We haven't tracked her down yet, nor have we located the people in the Bank looking the other way.'

Nic nodded. 'Agreed, but once we take Matt down, they will be around the place looking for a saviour, and that's where Anya might need to come in. That's the next stage if needed.'

Rose smiled. 'Then Anya goes back to Melbourne, and we're off to Hawaii to catch up with Jefferson, Eva and Emme.' Nic smiled. 'Well, not quite, but something happening might involve travel to Fiji and maybe North America. Are you guys interested? I think that's definitely, maybe overseas.'

'Stop teasing us. Yes, we are in, and yes, Fiji is overseas. Rose and I have even bought some new swimwear for it.'

'OK, great, I look forward to seeing it on my Credit Card statement. I'll email you the script, and we'll meet back here at one on Saturday to call Matt. I'll send him an email to give him the heads-up that you will be calling. I won't be on the call, as I'll be out of the state. See you then.'

He saluted, and they walked away, then turned back at Sandy and called out: 'Oh, what do we wear Nic? We will be ringing from Hamilton Island after all and don't have any of the latest resort wear, do we?'

'OK, go to Sea Folly in James Street, Fortitude Valley, and pick up some outfits for the show. Ensure you get the receipts. I need them for my files.'

'We know you don't do paperwork.'

'Yep, there is that. I was testing out the microphone

as you're still wearing the earbuds. Can I have them back now, please?'

At almost 1 p.m. Saturday, Anya and the crew made the final touches to the shelving and hanging racks. 'Nic says it has to be sparse. Nothing much needs to be on things, so boxes, plastic wrapping and unopened stuff are the keys.'

Rose nodded. 'Have you seen Nic? We managed to take pictures of Dog and had them printed off at Officeworks. We did a couple of sizes to see which suits the shot best.' Anya nodded. 'He's talking to the sound techs. The last thing we need is for the link to fail, and we have to ensure that whatever is happening in Hamilton Island can happen here, too. If it rains there, we have to make it rain here. Fortunately, the forecast is sunny, but we must prepare for all contingencies.'

Nic came over. 'Ten minutes to show time, guys. Everyone takes their place. Sound guys, start your checks, please. Lighting, get things moving. Rose and Sandy, take your seats, and we'll set you up.'

They sat down, and Nic did a sound check with the earplugs. 'Remember, don't turn your heads unless you have to. The vision will be evident, and he might just be able to see your earbuds. Is that what you are wearing? Wow, this is nerve-wracking for me. I'm not in total control.'

'Nic.'

'Yes, Sandy,'

'Breathe. We don't like seeing you stressed. Just leave everything to us, your capable companions.'

'Thanks. Two minutes, everyone.'

The final lighting was done, Dog's picture was selected and framed into the shot, the sound was checked, and they uploaded the link: 'Hello, Matt, are you there?'

'Yes, wow, this is a great link. It's almost that you are in the next suburb instead of being about nine hundred kilometres away, on Hamilton Island.'

'Are you in your office at Ipswich, Matt?'

'No, Sandy. I'm at our Head Office. How's it going? By the way, can you lift the iPad and show me around the shop?'

Rose looked towards Nic; he shook his head, then raised his hands and mouthed: *'No, it's in a cradle and can't be moved.'* Rose leaned out of the shot and mouthed back to him, tapping her earbuds. 'Speak, Nic, we can hear you.' Nic gave the double thumbs up.

Matt leaned toward the screen. 'Where did you go, Rose? And what is that behind you? It looks like a fluffy dog or something?'

'That's our Maine Coon Cat; we call him Dog. We had to leave him at home in Brisbane. We picked him up at the pound about ten years ago. He was a little kitten then but grew into a great fluffy ....'

Rose saw Nic shaking his head. 'Hey Matt, sorry we don't have much time. Did you hear from Sandy's husband, Nicklas Frank? He told us that he'd sent the forms to you for our loan application on Friday morning. Did you get them?'

'Yes, everything looks good, but I have to determine whether we can do the loan using Sandra's property at West End. I have done a title search, and there is a mortgage already, but you didn't declare a loan against it.' Sandy looked for direction from Nic; he was rolling his hands and nodding, and they heard him softly speaking through the earbuds: '*Keep him talking. Get a commitment from him regarding the timeline.*' Rose continued: 'Sandy doesn't have any loans at the moment, Matt. Everything was paid out when her grandmother passed away, and she paid off the house. It might be an old mortgage or something Nicklas has taken out without her knowing, as there's a bit of that going around Matt.'

Rose heard Nic in her ear again. '*Don't go there, Rose.*'

'What's that, Rose? I didn't quite catch it?'

'Nothing, Matt. How long will it take for you to approve the loan and for us to access some money?'

'Well, subject to Credit Checks and validation of the documents, the loan is already approved as I have the authority to do so. I'll send another form for Nicklas and Sandra to sign, and we'll lend up to eighty per cent of the property. How about a fit-out Loan of seventy-five thousand and an Overdraft, too? On top of that, we'll give you an equity home loan of another two hundred just against the property's value.

You don't have to use it, however. How does that all sound?'

Sandy nodded. 'Good, but can we have an advance on the loan now instead of waiting a few weeks?'

'Sure, I can do that too. Sandra, I'll need Nicklas to come into the Bank to complete a hundred-point identification, but once the account is opened, I'll immediately put an Overdraft Limit on it. I love the cat, by the way. My father used to have one like that; we called it Buster, as it used to bust everything up.'

Nic started twirling his finger to indicate that they should begin winding it up, and then he heard a siren. It was a fire truck off in the distance, and Matt had heard it, too. 'Hey guys, can you hear that? There must be a fire somewhere. Funny as the same sounding siren is coming through your Zoom call too.'

Nic signalled to terminate the call, but Sandy managed one more quip. 'Hey Matt, it's Sandy here. Have you ever been to my place at West End?'

The Zoom link then went blank.

CHAPTER 19

'Do you think I blew it? I couldn't hold out any longer. It's my house, and he has no right to play with my life.' Sandy turned away, and Rose comforted her.

Nic took a breath. 'I don't know yet, and I wouldn't know how to feel about all this either. It could have gone awry, but you played it as I expected. You guys are getting good at all this stuff. Thanks.'

Anya came over to them. 'Where to from here? Do you think he was where he said he was? We heard the fire siren, too. He must have been close, don't you think?'

'I have my tech guys working on the background. He was definitely in an office around here somewhere. Their Head Office is on Wickham Street in the Valley.'

Nic looked over to his geeks who were working on the vision, and one of them called him over. 'He's definitely in Fortitude Valley. We can see the McWhirter's building in the left corner. I know the building. He has his back on the street. We can work out the floor at the office. He's probably on the third floor.'

Nic nodded. 'Anya, can you call the Community

Bank Security Operations Centre? They should have a record of his security card scan showing he's entered the building and onto the third floor.'

Anya walked away, made the call, and then returned moments later. 'Yes, he entered the building at twelve-thirty, went to the third floor and hasn't come back down yet.'

Nic corralled the troops together, and the posse drove to the Community Bank Head Office. It would take less than fifteen minutes from where they were. Anya, Rose, Sandy and three others were all squished into the Chrysler 300C. Nic found a park out the front and slapped an *'Active Police Business'* sign on the car's front window.

Rose looked at it. 'That's not a real sign, surely, Nic? I mean, it's handwritten. Anybody could do that.'

'Yep, but it still works.'

They met two Community Bank Security Officers at the Bank's Head Office and were let in. The Officers looked at Sandy and Rose dressed in their resort wear but said nothing. Nic grinned.

'Hi, I'm Brady, and this is Erin. We've been briefed as to what this is about. Let's get the show on the road.'

Nic then took control. 'Let's split up; remember, we can't arrest or detain him against his will. All we can do is convince him to give up, and we wait for the Police. It could be simple, or it could get ugly. He isn't a big man, but he may be armed. We don't know. Play it cool, keep safe, and look out for each other.'

Anya nodded. 'Thanks, Nic. Let's split into two groups. Our group will go up in the lifts. And Nic, you take the others into the stairwell. I've just received a text update from Security Ops, and he hasn't left the floor yet.' Her group then headed for the lifts. Nic called out. 'Wait a moment before you move, Anya. I'll call you when we're at the third-floor fire door.'

Nic led his group to the stairwell and quietly went up the three flights. They reached the floor door, and he held up his hand to indicate his group to stop. He tried the door handle, and it was unlocked. He called Anya on his mobile, but there was no connection. 'Damn it, guys, we're in a cement bunker; I can't get her. They're on their own.'

Meanwhile, as Anya hadn't heard from Nic, she decided to move anyway. They were squished in the small lift, and anxious, heavy breathing was happening. 'How are you guys doing?' looking over to Rose and Sandy.

'I don't know about Rose, but I didn't think this through. Without him, we wouldn't have been this close to any of Nic's criminals. Rose did bash one over the head with an iPad, though.'

Rose looked over to one of Nic's geek people with them. He had headphones over his ears, his eyes closed, and he swayed his head with the beat of whatever he was listening to, then looked at Brady for confirmation.

'Hey, don't look at me. I was just out for a coffee, and they told me to let you guys in. It's my second day.'

'OK, so we're Brady's Bunch without an Alice unless one of you wants to step up. Nic was supposed to call when he got to the third-floor door.'

Brady shook his head. 'His phone won't work in there, Anya. It's a black spot due to the older style of cement building construction. I would say we're on our own.' The lift pinged as they arrived on the 3rd floor.

Brady stepped out first, followed by the geek who still hadn't removed his headphones, and then the three women. Nic and his posse weren't there. Rose whispered, 'Damn you, Nic.'

Meanwhile, Nic opened the door just a crack and heard the lift ping. 'We have to get out there, guys'. He leaned into the door more, but it wouldn't move. After counting his shoulder against the door again, he realised something was preventing it from opening. Taking his phone from his pocket, Nic slipped it through the space, took a photo, and viewed the result: A two-door wooden cabinet wedged against the bottom of the door. It was face down on the floor.

Nic then cautiously looked through the crack and saw that Anya's posse had exited the lift. He knew that Anya was coming in from the northern side, so at least that was in their favour, as Matt Seaford was most likely in one of the southern side offices, if still there. Nic looked back to his group for inspiration. 'Any ideas? We have to get this cabinet moved.'

One of the younger crew looked at him. 'Nic, tell me if I am out of place, but I think I have an idea.'

'Anything, mate. What have you got?'

'The second floor. Why don't we go down there and come back up in the lift.'

'You're on. Remind me to give you a bonus when this is all over.' Nic's group hustled down to the second floor and opened the door. They went directly to the lifts and arrived back on the third floor.

Fortunately, as Anya's crew had moved out of vision, Nic assumed they were now going past the southern side offices. He risked the text and sent her a message: 'Stop. We're here. Come back.'

Anya read it, put her hand up, and told her group to backtrack.

They had only just entered the southern side office area, and Nic was relieved when he saw them coming back towards him. 'Ok, this is how we are going to run it. We'll split into threes. I'll take Rose and Sandy. Brady, you take the geek and Anya. Erin, you go with the other two. Take it very slowly and carefully, and walk away if necessary. He hasn't left yet, so he has to be in here somewhere.'

Erin looked at Nic. 'Um, I have a Taser, Nic; it's my own, but I don't think I should have it. Do you want it?' She pulled it from the holster. 'It's only for show as it doesn't hold a charge.'

'I don't trust those things. Please remove it and leave it on that cabinet by the fire door. I'm surprised you're permitted to carry. We'll collect it later.'

The groups split up and went through the corridors and offices cautiously and carefully, and after circling back around, there was nothing. Matt was gone.

Sandy addressed the group. 'Hey, I know what office he uses, though, as there was a picture of our cat in the office. Also, piles of unopened mail addressed to different people 'C/- Matt Steele, Community Bank Head Office''.

'Yep, that's where I reckon he made the call from earlier too. It was also the background shot with the McWhirter's building lined up. But where did he go? We've searched every office, but there's nowhere for him to hide, nothing large enough. I reckon he must have another way of getting out. Let's get out of here, then. Leave it for Erin and Brady to wind it up.'

The seven left Erin and Brady on the third floor and caught the lift to the ground. Sandy stopped. 'Damn it, Nic, I don't want him to have a picture of our Dog in his office. Can I go and get it? Erin and Brady would still be up there anyway.'

'No worries, Sandy. Just let them know you're back on the floor when you leave. We'll wait for you down here.'

Sandy took the lift up to the third floor and

announced loudly that she was stepping out from the doors, but Erin and Brady weren't there to greet her. Then she noticed that a wooden cabinet had been moved from being abutted against the fire door. It didn't have a lid or a base. It was just a four-sided empty box, so she moved towards it.

'Erin, Brady, where are you? I've returned to get the stupid picture that the stupid man has in his office.' Sandy heard a noise behind her and turned around. It was Matt Seaford, and he wasn't alone. A man about the same age, dressed in an almost matching outfit, stood beside him. The men both placed their shoulder bags onto the floor.

'Hello, Sandra Fraser. This is my partner, Joe. He's pleased to meet you, too.'

Sandy went to step back but realised it was only towards the lifts and wouldn't be quick enough to get there, so she took a deep breath, crossed her arms over her chest, and with her 1.8m frame towered over the two shorter men. 'Hello, Matt. It's nice to meet you too, Joe. I am one of Matt's new clients. I own that Maine Coon cat that he has a picture of in his office. Didn't it used to belong to your father?'

'Shut up, Sandy. That damn cat killed him. It made him crash his car. I was glad when Uncle Bill finally got rid of it. He told me he had it put down, but he kept all those stupid pictures around and then used it as his stupid mascot for his stupid Ice Hockey Team.'

'Nope, it lives and breathes at my place, but you

already know that, Matt. You've been there, and I have the photos to prove it. What's with stealing my property details from the title certificate on my den? That was nasty of you.'

'That wasn't me, you dumb woman; it was the stupid woman that I lent the fifteen thousand dollars to. I didn't think it was you; she was too short, and I thought you were much prettier, but she had your ID and property title details, so I gave her the loan anyway. She told me she had been in a car accident and would pay the loan off when the claim came through. She lied to me, and then you turned up with your silly story about 'The She Shed.''

'Hey, some people commit fraud, Matt, but they all get caught in the end, something to do with having a thorn in their side.'

'Hilarious Sandy, Nic Thorn, what a doofus. When I gave my talk at the AFA thing, he must have thought I was mad, but I'm not going down without a fight. If you see him again, tell that to your superhero wanna-be, Nic Thorn. I can still make all this work. You're just making me mad.'

Sandy stood firm. 'No, Matt, Nic knows you're already mad. So, the longer you keep me here, the madder Nic gets, and you don't want to get him mad. He kills people. Matt especially likes killing weedy little bank lenders.' Sandy looked at Joe. 'And I hope you, not a bank lender too, as he'd make that a double tap.'

Joe looked at Sandy, then at Matt. 'Come on, Matty.

Let's get out of here. You've taken care of Brady and Erin. It was so funny when we leapt out at them when they moved the cabinet, and then you hit them with the tire iron. I don't think they will be waking up very soon.'

Joe then revealed the iron bar behind his back and hefted it in his hands. 'We can either do this quietly or our way, we don't care. Start moving. We're taking the stairs.'

Sandy considered her options as they pushed her towards the stairs, then noticed Erin's Taser gun was on the ground and reached for it. The men let her pick it up. 'Erin said it doesn't charge. So what will you do, rub it on the carpet, then throw it at us?' Matt opened the fire door and pushed her through, and then Joe stepped through to go in front of her. 'Move, Sandy.' Sandy felt tears coming, held them in, and heard the lift ping behind her.

'Sandy, where are you?' It was Nic. 'Over here by the stairs. I found Matt, who has a tender lender lover with him, too.' Sandy then put one of her Django and Juliette sandals in the middle of Joe's back and shoved him down the stairs. He went head over heels and crashed solidly into the wall at the next landing. He was out cold. Matt looked at her. 'That wasn't nice, Sandy.'

Sandy grinned. 'Well, this won't be either then, Matt.' Sandy pointed the Taser at him and pulled the trigger. Matt smirked at her, but the barbs shot out from the gun. One hit him in the face, the other in his neck, and the charge went off. He quivered, slobbered, shuddered in pain, and then slumped to the ground. Nic looked at Sandy. Nic looked down at him. 'You can take your finger off the trigger. I think that he's got the point.'

Sandy released her finger and dropped the Taser. Matt, all the while, kept shaking with electric pulses coursing through his body. 'How long before he stops doing that? It's creeping me out.'

'I have no idea. That's something Nic Thorn doesn't know.'

'So, what brought you up here? I mean, did you miss me already?'

'Well, when we were downstairs, Erin confessed that she had lied as the Taser was in working order, so I came up to collect it. They can be dangerous, you know.'

Sandy looked at Nic, then started to move quickly towards him. They held each other, and Sandy began to cry. The lift pinged again, and some of the other crew came out. Sandy and Nic moved apart. 'He was in the cupboard, Rose. It didn't have a top on it, and that's how they would get out. They pushed on the fire door and created a space to crawl out. He wasn't alone in there either; he had a little friend with him. It must have been squeezy in there, but they are both well and out of the closet now. Brady and Erin are around here somewhere, too. The closet men jumped on them when they were shifting the cupboard. Matt smashed them with a tire iron.'

'I've found them.' It was a call out from Anya. 'Ambulance is on the way too. What about the other guy, Sandy? Where is he?'

'Staring at something in the stairwell, Anya. Maybe a wall or maybe his eyelids? The last time I saw him, he didn't look so well, but don't call a second Ambulance just yet, please, Anya.'

Nic shook his head. 'He may be really hurt, Sandy. Besides this thing with the banks and the AFA, Nic Thorn and Co will have a big reward payout. You and Rose are the Co., by the way.'

Sandy sighed. 'Do I get my house back, Nic?'

'Yep, Anya has a lead on the woman who lodged the mortgage too. So, let's go back home, or better yet, how about you take a couple of nights R & R at the Palazzo Versace down the coast?'

'Sorry, but I have to feed Dog first and hug him for bringing all of this down, but we'll take you up on that. Rose and I need to experience their soft couches. Can we get a room with a waterbed, too?'

'Don't push your luck, Annie Oakley. Good shot, by the way.'

'He was less than a meter away from me.'

'That's the point. You held your nerve and shot him anyway, which takes courage.'

The ambulance officers placed Erin and Brady on gurneys and removed them, then the Police arrived, and as the offenders were now both conscious, both were waiting to be put into separate police wagons. Joe started spilling the beans like a blubbering jellyfish, and they didn't even have to get him back to the watch house before confessing to his role in the loan scams.

'Can I see him? Can I please speak to Matt, Officer Deakin? Do you think we will be going to jail?'

The arresting Officer looked at him. 'Better getter a lawyer, son, better get a real good one.'

Rose overheard and looked at Nic. 'Hey, he just quoted The Cruel Sea, Nic.'

'Nope, that was .....My god, Rose, you're right.'

CHAPTER 20

Rose and Sandy were standing on their balcony at the Palazzo Versace on the Gold Coast. It was around 10 a.m. Rose's and Sandy's phone rang. 'Hi, Nic. Do you know how early it is? We're in a different time zone down here.'

'You're still in Queensland, guys.'

'Yes, but it's holiday time. What can we do for you?'

'Anya has finished things up, so you can return if you like. She was missing her little man and wanted to get back home. I asked her about her life partner, and she told me he was long gone but is managing with the help of her Mum. I dropped five thousand into her Bank account to thank her for keeping you under control. Hope you didn't mind.'

'Good work, Nic. Did you catch up with Sandy's doppelganger? I assume the mortgage is coming off her house, and the Debt Collection Agency has dropped the matter, too?'

'Well, not quite, but it's still in motion. As for the woman, she has bobbed up in other loans that went across Matt's desk, but it was only your loan that she visited his office to do the signup. The rest have been matched with handwriting samples, but he has let her get away with a lot of money. She is still in the wind.'

'What about the inside person at Community Bank? Did Anya track them down?'

'Yep, it turned out to be Matt's immediate Line Manager. He was the same one in charge when Matt Steele was around, too. It sounds like he will keep his job; maybe he will be demoted sideways, but that's not our concern anymore. It's a Fraud Squad matter now.'

'So, what did you ring for? Has something else come up? The overseas Fiji thing?'

'Nope, but we might catch up with Anya again soon.'

'She lives in Melbourne, Nic.'

'Yep, that is where we are going, so brush up on your French, Rose. I need you to be a waitress in a French immersion restaurant at the New Crowd Casino. Are you up for that?'

'Oui.'

'Ah Rose, Mon petit chou chou.'

'Nic, you don't speak French, do you?'

'Non. Pour Quoi?'

'Well, you just called me a little cabbage.'

Keep reading for an excerpt from the next adventures of Nic Thorn and Associates: 'Three French Bens'

-

<u>Three French Bens</u>

Rosemary Palmer stood in the middle of a large 360° wrap-around steel counter, surrounded by dead fish. *'Damn you, Nic Thorn, I hate the smell of fish.'* Rose held a bent arm to her nose, trying to spare herself from the soggy, sweet, icy smell. She was the only one in the shop looking forward to finishing her shift within half an hour. Nic Thorn, her business partner and mentor, had just left to collect another container of ice to throw onto the open shelves to keep everything fresh.

Outside, it was another sunny, hot, and humid day in Brisbane, and the throng of sounds from the

Rocklea Markets wafted through the shop walls, but the fish business was slow today. The shop door opened, and Sandy, Rose's BFF, came in to collect her. 'Geez, Rose, it's a stinker out there today and, by the smell of it, not much better in here either.'

'Very funny, Sandy. No one buys fresh fish in Brisbane on these hot days without bringing an esky. Who knew? We can wrap it up as tightly as possible, but you leave it in the hot car, even for a short time, and the stinky, hot, fishy smell stays with you for a week. At least the feral cats follow you around, though.'

'Well, about that, Rose, tomorrow we're supposed to be heading down to Melbourne to look into this Three French Bens Restaurant thing with Nic, but I don't think I'll be going now. Dog has been catnapped, well, gone missing anyway. He didn't come in for his kitty dins this morning, and nothing stands in the way of our Maine Coon cat and his breakfast.'

'Did you check with Dave next door?'

'Not yet, but Dave told me that Dog has been off his food a bit. The cat won't touch anything that smells of fish, and that's all he had to feed him.'

Nic returned to the shop, pushing the trolley of plastic tubs full of ice, and wheeled it past Sandy. 'Hey Sandy, you smell nice. Still having those three showers when you return from the early morning fish deliveries?'

'Yep, but it still doesn't help.'

Nic tipped the ice into the open troughs. 'You

know, Rose, after three weeks of doing this, I can hardly smell the dead fish, but then again, I have been breathing through my mouth for most of the time anyway.'

'Damn you, Nic.'

For more reading from the Nic Thorn and Associates series of capers, enjoy the following stories:

One Tricked Phoney

-

Rose needed a +1, but not for the usual wedding/party. She was going to a funeral and needed a quiet, unassuming type. Rose and her BFF Sandy had time on their hands and soon found Nic would fill the void. He coerces them into his madcap investigations of scams, frauds, and misunderstandings. These modern-day adventures lead them from one lively caper to another, involving portrait provenance, invoice inaccuracy, and a recycler's relapse, on their travels from Brisbane, Adelaide, to the SA border.

Three French Bens

Nic's friend, Benoit Trudeau, is one-third of the 'Three French Bens' at the New Crowd Casino in Melbourne. He has just bought into a high-end restaurant, so he calls Nic's Team in to have a look, as the numbers look fishy, and they might have to go angling for the truth. Nic and his crew then head to Rockhampton to help the Queensland Department of Agriculture look into some cattle duffing, as apparently, it's heard a lot up that way. Finally, Sandy has to deal with an old school friend, or is that a fiend that has been taking a loan from her, at her expense?

<u>Four brooding Birds</u>

-

The Australian Department of Agriculture often deals with snakes and adders, and this time, Nic and the team are brought in to investigate reptile smuggling in Western Australia. While over there, the team also finds a fraudster drinking from the sweet success of Margaret River wines. Then, a short time later, they must look into genuine budgie smugglers, west of the New South Wales border.

<u>Five Mouldy Bins</u>

-

It's Christmas in July, and the Department of Health in Brisbane is concerned that someone may be stuffing their stockings with ill-gotten gains, so Nic and the team are brought in to bring it to a head – reindeer style. Meanwhile, Sandy and Rose meet up with their 'friend' Dimond, who needs to lease a new rental property for her family in Brisbane. Then, the team gets involved in a diamond scam, and the resolution could be clear-cut, but getting stranded in Dubai on the way to South Africa was never in the plan.

Six Geezers Lying

The team is back in Adelaide as car insurance companies are driven up the wall by bogus claims and 'accidents'. Then, one of the national restaurant chains puts together a competition so easy that anyone can win, but prizes are being awarded even before the competition is finished. The team then gets involved in an art scam back in Brisbane, and Rose's Father is in the middle of it. Art is not always art, depending on your point of view, but fraud is always fraud.

Seven hapless Hoops

This time, the team heads to Ouyen, in Victoria, as one of Nic's old school friends calls upon him to locate his missing wife; whilst this is not generally within the scope of what they do, it is too close to home for Nic not to be in the right place to investigate. Rose and Driver go into solo mode to find a missing car in Mildura, and a horse racing scam is gathering pace on Kangaroo Island, off the coast of Adelaide, and in Nic's line of business, a lot of that is going around, and around.

Author's Biography:

The author is a former long-term banker by profession and worked within the Bank's Credit Card Fraud Team, where he obtained a Private Investigators License. There are seven other completed titles in the ten-book series awaiting publication, and the eighth novel, ' Eight Dave's are Weak' is currently underway.

The author resides between Adelaide, South Australia, and the Sunshine Coast, Queensland. He has been fortunate to have visited many places and enjoys including them in these stories.

In November 2020, the first novel in the Nic Thorn Caper series: 'One Jaded Rose' was published with the assistance of Tellwell Books, Canada.

In November 2022, the author won an award from Wakefield Press, Adelaide for his short story: ' Car on a Hill'.

www.ingramcontent.com/pod-product-compliance
Lightning Source LLC
Chambersburg PA
CBHW020509120726
47904CB00003B/759